D1710971

Crack in the Curtain

Selatin Softa

Selatin Softa

ISBN-13: 978-0692260777

www.selatinsofta.com

Cover Photograph by Selatin Softa

Interior Photograph Contributed by Selatin Softa

While this is a work of fiction, the story is based on the real events of the forceful name change campaign conducted by the Bulgarian Communist Party against the Turks in Bulgaria from 1984 to 1985.

Acknowledgements

First of all, I'd like to thank my cherished love, my wife, Amy, for her insight during the writing of this novel. I'm very grateful for her patience in putting up with my tantrums and for all her indispensable help.

The people of Krumovgrad and the surrounding villages were the inspiration for this story. My Bulgarian teachers, too, inspired me.

Thanks to Jan McDonald for her kind help in making grammatical changes as she read through my book.

I am so appreciative of my grandmother, Isman, and my father, Ismail, for their inspiration and their kindness. Because of them, I was brought up to appreciate my own culture.

My brother, Sabahtin, loved Shakespeare, read all the time, and managed to instill a love of literature in me, too. He was eleven years older than I, but I followed in his footsteps in reading all the books he owned or borrowed from the library. I was his "mini-me."

I am grateful to Christine Gilroy for all her contributions and all her knowledge brought to the book.

Chapter 1

Late Autumn, 1984

My heart was breaking, but I did not have a choice if I wanted to live. It was either surrender and risk being killed or spend years, maybe the rest of my life, in prison or a death camp — or flee the country and live free, but alone.

On this, my last night in my village, my home, I knew I would never experience our old house or the village like this again, with the sounds of nature and the animals, and people happily anticipating another busy summer day.

Mustafa and I left our village with a small bag of food, clothes, folding knife and pliers. As the thunderstorm ended, we rode Lightning fast on remote shepherd trails, south toward the border. We could not use the roads, or even travel close to the roads for fear of being seen by police. Hope and fear gripped my heart, and I realized I had put all our families' lives in danger, Mustafa's, Ömer's, and mine. There was no easy way to hide a horse and its riders, and police looking for us would have no problem spotting us from a distance.

Suddenly in the distance I heard the faint noise of an engine, louder than a police truck and high in the sky — a military helicopter approaching fast. My heart hammered as I looked for a place to hide, but there was not a single tree or bush or cave anywhere. I spurred Lightning to a full gallop and we flew across the field. I buried my face in Lightning's thick mane to cut wind resistance, and Mustafa leaned on my back, but we were no match for the speed of the helicopter which descended upon us like an angry eagle. The soldiers opened fire and bullets whooshed by us as I steered Lightning zigzag to a dry riverbed of small stones. Lightning lost his balance and we all collapsed in a big cloud of dust and stones.

The helicopter ominously turned in a circle over us, sure they had hit us, stirring up a big cloud of dust that hid us. I undid Lightning's headstall and saddle fast and turned him loose. I knew he would find his way home. As the helicopter approached the ground, its tail rotor hit a tree and broke into pieces. The helicopter spun violently and crashed into the ground, causing the earth to shake from the impact. The main rotor broke into pieces that were flung all over the surrounding area. Mustafa and I were knocked down from the shock wave as the helicopter exploded and everything caught fire. There was no way any of our attackers could have survived the horrible accident.

Chapter 2

Early Summer, 1984

My life was not always full of pain and loss. I did not know in the beginning that my life would consist of continually overcoming obstacles. But those obstacles shaped me into the man I am today. They were simply a record of events that happened and influenced my life. I cannot forget them. My story, in some ways, is the story of the ethnic Turks living in Bulgaria, because it is something that all of us lived through. I remember the events of 1984 as if they happened yesterday.

I have carried the guilt and remorse with me for years, since that fateful black fall night of 1984 when Mustafa and I fled for the cold border of the notorious Iron Curtain, in no man's land between Bulgaria and Greece. From that day, I have blamed myself and the evil Communist regime of Bulgaria for leaving us no other option, except escape, to survive.

Mustafa had said he didn't want to live in Bulgaria anymore, but I always had this nagging feeling that he followed me only because he didn't want me to cross the border by myself.

Mustafa and I, as well as the rest of the ethnic Turks in Bulgaria, lived simple, peaceful existences prior to 1984. We had no opposition to the ruling Communist regime, for it was an entity far removed from our sleepy little villages of southern Bulgaria in the eastern Rhodope Mountains. We minded our business and worked hard for little pay in the tobacco fields of the region. Our lives were simple and poor, but free of political turmoil; politics was often the last thing on our minds. With nothing to compare ourselves to, we didn't realize how poor we were. We were trapped in the East European Communist bloc at the very edge of southeastern Europe, very close to member countries of the Western world — Greece to the south, and Turkey to the southeast. We also were on the geographical divide, the fault line, of two great religions: Islam and Eastern Orthodox Christianity.

I was born 17 years before the start of the name change campaign of 1984. My parents named me Osman after my great-grandfather, who was named for his grandfather. The name Osman, passed down in my family for many generations, was a Turkish name, the name of the founder of the great Ottoman Empire. My appearance was typical for many of the Turks from this area; I was medium build with black hair, muscular from all the hard work in the tobacco fields surrounding my town, and strong from the healthy food that came with life here in my small village.

I lived with my parents in a house built in the 1940s by my grandparents in the village of Çaliköy (cha-la-koy), situated in the south central part of

Bulgaria. Çalıköy was the name given by the Turkish population for the village. Of course, the village had a Bulgarian name, too — Starichal. The people living there were ethnic Turks, so no one used the Bulgarian version. It was used only for official papers.

The village was a small hamlet when it was founded, when this area of Bulgaria was part of the Ottoman Empire. After the Balkan Wars, the Ottoman Empire lost the region to Bulgaria. As the borders were redrawn, the area heavily populated with ethnic Turks ended up becoming the southeastern part of Bulgaria. In all of Bulgaria there were hundreds of thousands of ethnic Turks working and living peaceful lives.

Our home was a simple structure of two stories, built of rectangular blocks cut from the surrounding mountain with the blocks connected with mortar. The first floor was used as a barn for the storage of hay. The second floor was accessible only by an outside stone stairway made from large rectangular stones cut wider and longer so people could easily step onto them. At the top of the stairs was a small landing, and there you would find the door to the living quarters of the house. The entrance door led into a wide foyer, part of which was used as a kitchen with a big cupboard with shelves built by my father on every wall. The shelves were filled with countless jars of preserved tomatoes, peppers, peaches, apricots, pears, and lamb meat in the summer and fall. Most of the shelves would be empty by late spring, their contents used in cooking or eaten during the winter.

The interior of the house was plastered with white and gray clay found in the local field. The smooth, wide walls and gray mud plaster kept the house warm during the cold Balkan winters and cool during the long and hot summers. On the top of the cupboard was one of our latest acquisitions, a small electric hotplate. My parents purchased it after the electrification of the village during the 1970s. Next to the cupboard was the second addition to the house, a small refrigerator. In the corner my mother kept the butter churn, which resembled the barrel of a cannon — it just spat butter instead of shells. There was also a small wood barrel filled with turşu, pickled vegetables, sitting next to a large bag of flour used by my mother to make pancakes and bread. There were wide windows looking out at the front of the house and a narrow one on the side of the foyer. The room was flooded with light, so everything was easily seen during the day. Between the windows in the outer wall of the foyer was the only sink in the house, with a small container of water hanging over it, and gravity fed the water through a small faucet at the bottom. We refilled the water with copper buckets stored on a shelf on the opposite wall. Before we got running water in the front of the house, sometime in the 1980s, we had to carry all the water we used for drinking in the kitchen and bath from a single, big water fountain in the center of the village. All this water-carrying business was done mainly by the women of the village. Two copper water buckets were hung on the bakır ağaç, a slightly curved wooden yoke put onto the shoulders for the walk back to the house.

There were three doors that led from the foyer to the rest of the house. One door led to the dining room which was also used by my parents as a bedroom. Another room was mine, with a bed and small cabinet that held my school supplies. The third and last room used to belong to my grandparents, my father's parents, but was used as a guest room after they passed away. In that room was the small hamam, a shower. The attic of the house, where tobacco was kept, was accessible through an opening in the ceiling. The faint smell of the leaves lingered throughout the house.

I remember during my youth going to the tobacco fields early in the morning before dawn and seeing the sun rise in the gently curving hills of eastern Rhodope Mountains, covered with the bright green carpet of the tobacco fields. With the breaking of the dawn, the promise of a new beautiful, peaceful day, a bountiful tobacco harvest was anticipated by my family and all the villagers. With it and the inevitable crowing of the roosters, life awakened everywhere, simple, elemental, pristine, and primordial. The sun's light and warmth covered the ruins of many old Byzantine castles scattered through the hills. Life in this mountain had been going on in this cycle since time immemorial.

In the spring, people got ready to plant tobacco, growing seeds to small plants in small hothouses to plant early in the summer. In the second half of summer the tobacco was finally collected, then dried until late fall. Later in the fall and early winter, the tobacco was processed into big square bales, which my father and I would store in the attic of our home.

I felt as if my parents, all the villagers and I were a part of this never-ending cycle. We lived with the peace and beauty of this place and an inner peace that we thought, and anticipated, would continue indefinitely. The logical expectation was that I would continue working tobacco like my parents and grandparents.

I remember my parents sitting under the big grapevine in the front of the house, which provided nice shade most of the day during summer. Their image was imprinted in my mind like a picture or painting, part of time and space preserved forever, a slice of their life. They strung tobacco using big needles. They sat on soft cushions my mother made from wool and cloth. She always wore her shalwar of baggy pants, a shirt made from the same material, and a colorful headscarf. My father was dressed in simple black or blue work pants and a bright colored shirt. They would sit a few feet apart and lean slightly toward each other as if they belonged together. Healthy, but their faces aged prematurely from the hard work in the tobacco fields and exposure to the elements in the long hot summers and cold winters in the mountains.

The summer nights of the Rhodope Mountains were wonderful in my village. I remember the warm gentle breeze caressing my skin. Sometimes with Mustafa, sometimes alone, I spent time out in the big meadow planted with alfalfa behind the village, breathing in the intoxicating smell of wildflowers and listening to the gentle whisper of the summer breeze through the almond, linden, and tall poplar trees by the water fountain on the edge of a tall hill. We would hear the occasional cry of an owl, the song of a thousand crickets, or an occasional frog.

The narrow cobblestone-paved streets were not lit at night, except for the few lights that people mounted on the outer walls of their houses to light their front yards after the electrification of the village. The meadow of alfalfa behind the village, however, was lit only by the light of the moon and stars. After small talk about mundane things in village life, we would fall silent and lie among the soft, fragrant plants and stare at the sky. Due to the lack of artificial light, we could clearly see countless stars shimmering like precious stones in the vast dome above us. We would find the Big Dipper and Small Dipper and stare at the moon, which looked like a huge molten iron circle. The darkened hills surrounding the village came to life like mythical figures. I felt connected not only to the people and animals in the village, but to the whole Earth. I felt merged with the sky and whole universe. I was the universe and the universe was me.

I would entertain the thought that part of me would somehow exist forever in that vast sky, among the countless stars. I could not fathom the idea that our lives or the life of one of us could end suddenly. It was an impossibility under the eternal shimmer of the night stars. Stillness would ease over me and I would just enjoy the beauty of nature and the night sky in peace and happiness. I felt, and believed, that I, and all people of Earth, were somehow connected and nurtured good will toward each other, and the world was not a threatening place. The sky was a father figure watching over me with its many stars and moon, and the Earth was the mother who took care of me, feeding me and holding me gently in her embrace.

When the summer was saying hello to autumn by changing the lush green leaves of trees and leftover leaves of tobacco plants in the fields to shades of gold, I knew my time to go back to school was swiftly approaching. The gold and brown leaves of the trees fell one by one, silently and unnoticeably, like our days slipping by one by one, and wind dispersed them into the void. All the swallows that built nests under the roof of our house departed quietly to the south, to northern Africa, and I felt orphaned. A little sadness set in, because the long warm summer was a memory and cooler northern winds foretold the coming of cold winter. I had to say goodbye to my village life and my friends and go to school in Krumovgrad, or Koşukavak (ko-shoo-ka-vak) as we call it in Turkish, the kasaba, the town.

I had about one week left until school started in September. Until then I would have time to go to the marketplace in Krumovgrad on Friday. I would even have time to ride our neighbor's horse Lightning on Sunday. That same afternoon, I would travel to Krumovgrad for the school year.

Seasons changed gently here in the eastern Rhodope Mountains and they were mainly gentle all throughout the year. Maybe that's why this part of the world was called the Cradle of Ancient Civilization and became the foundation for modern Western civilization. I was living a happy, calm, uneventful life here, thinking that life would continue that way forever. I thought that the gathering storm of what we Turks uneasily called the name change campaign would somehow miss us.

But I was wrong.

Chapter 3

Hasan was our neighbor. We added to his name the term aga, which was a polite form used to address older males. He lived with his wife, Fidan; their children were grown and had moved to Kirdjali, a bigger city where they were factory workers. Hasan aga and Fidan were happiest when their children and grandchildren came to visit them for the Kurban Bayram, the Feast of Sacrifice celebration. Kurban Bayram was the best time of the year. People were nice to each other and a spirit of forgiveness prevailed. Kurban Bayram was the festival of sacrifice where every family, at least those who could afford to, would sacrifice a ram. Part of the meat would be collected and cooked in a big cauldron and everybody in the village would celebrate by participating in the big feast. The leftovers would be divided among the participants.

Hasan aga's house was located uphill from our house, on a slight slope. His house was similar to ours, just a bit larger and newer. There were few horses in the village, but Hasan aga owned the most handsome Arab horse of them all, Lightning. Arab horses had been widely used by the Ottoman cavalry. Unfortunately, with the ending of the great empire, the horsemanship lifestyle went with it, along with their majestic beasts.

Lightning was the fastest horse in the village. No other horse ever won in a competition against Lightning; he was always true to his name. He was fast and he was good looking, too; his shiny flank was deep brown like a chestnut. He had an expressive and lively look in his eyes. People who saw Lightning were fascinated by his beauty and energy.

Hasan aga was in his sixties and he didn't feel that he could continue to take Lightning for gallops anymore. He wanted somebody with more energy to ride the young stallion, somebody who would be a good match for the explosive energy of Lightning. I was Hasan aga's choice because he trusted me and liked me. He once said that he observed similarities between Lightning and me; he thought I, too, was energetic and fearless and had the spirit of a winner. Hasan aga had allowed me to ride Lightning those last few years and we developed a special bond between us. We understood each other with little verbal communication on my part.

The town name Koşukavak, or Krumovgrad in Bulgarian, derived from the time of the Ottoman Empire when there were horse races by the poplar trees by the river. In fact, the translation of Koşukavak was "horse race by the poplar trees." But this tradition was discouraged by the Bulgarian government and with the demise of the Ottoman Empire and its horses, unfortunately, this great tradition went into oblivion. But the memories of Hasan aga's father and my grandfather were intact and they would often talk about those times of racing horses.

Hasan aga was a slender man with deep wrinkles on his face as a result of exposure to sun and harsh weather in the tobacco fields. His arms and hands were muscular from the hard farm work. The fingers of his right hand were yellow from smoking tobacco all his life. Even though he was in his sixties he looked older. His face looked as though he knew a lot about life, and there was wisdom in his eyes.

There was a long-standing dispute between Hasan aga and Kanlı, who lived in the upper part of the village. Everybody knew about the fierce nature of Kanlı — his name even meant "bloody." They fought multiple times about a little stretch of land behind the village. To be more precise, they were unable to decide on the dividing line of two fields. I had heard that Kanlı, who was about Hasan aga's age or maybe a little younger, got involved in knife fights in his youth and he would win. But Hasan aga wasn't somebody to be sneered at, either. He was tough and he worked in the building of the Studen Kladenets dam, which was about five kilometers from the village. He became legendary for his toughness and hard work and was awarded prizes by the managers of the project and local Communist party leaders. People in the village were worried that this feud could end up with somebody getting hurt or even killed, "Allah korusun," or "God forbid" as villagers would say. So the services of the beloved peacemaker Ramazan hoca, priest and teacher in Ada, were requested for the two warring parties. Before every Kurban Bayram celebration, Ramazan hoca talked to both parties. Despite the fact that Ramazan hoca was trusted by both parties, neither one would budge. Everybody was disappointed that there was no peace between the two still, but we all kept hope and faith that things would be different next year.

Our family was like an extended family to Hasan aga. He didn't show emotion often, but he had the respect of our family. Usually Hasan aga and my father sat outside in a little makeshift seating area, with big logs used as stools and a really big one for a table, under the plum trees and the single big almond tree. The smell of that blooming almond in the spring was intoxicating. Life was not easy growing tobacco on mountain hills, but they didn't know any better. I sometimes heard Hasan aga and my father saying that life was fair. Their love for their families, religion, and land gave them faith that they could face life's challenges. Their power originated in their support for each other. In their busy lives, they did not have much time to stop and think about themselves. They were busy working and taking care of children, old relatives, animals, gardens, and houses. Their doors were wide open for all neighbors and they were free to visit each other when they needed to do so.

Hasan aga encouraged me to ride Lightning, and I thought that it would be good for Lightning to be ridden, too.

"You can take and ride Lightning," Hasan aga said one day, "but be careful not to get hurt, you or Lightning."

"Don't worry Hasan aga, I will take good care of Lightning. I will not let anything happen to him."

"You have to saddle him yourself, the saddle was in the barn." The barn was a simple stone structure next to the house. I went inside the enclosed area where Lightning was and he was very excited to see me. He ran toward me and started whinnying, knowing we would be going for a ride.

"Merhaba, hello, how are you doing today, handsome?" I got the blanket and saddle and put them on Lightning. He seemed not to mind being saddled because he did not move. With joy, I anticipated the ride outside the horse's pen. I got on Lightning's back and we moved slowly through a narrow road that led up to a plateau on the upper side of the village. The plateau was covered with grass and was long and level and suitable to run fast. It was nice to be above everything to see so far away. From the end of the plateau I was able to see the valley covered with big green tobacco plantations, the narrow winding road connecting Haskovo to Krumovgrad, and the small bus stop.

When we got to the plateau, I liked to go as fast as I could. The speed, the rushing wind, the sense of freedom, felt so good and so exhilarating, pretty much like flying. Lightning ran so fast, as though he'd been waiting for this moment a long time. I felt connected to Lightning, we were two parts of one whole, kindred spirits connected through a natural affinity. After running a couple of times across the plateau, I decided I would go to the small creek running below the village on the southern part between two hills. I thought that it would be more fun if I took somebody with me so I decided to take Mustafa with me. We could cool down in the small pool named Hasan Buguldu, which means Hasan drowned. We had a good swim in the warm clear water of the pool, but on our way back from the creek we were all tired. Both Mustafa and I were riding Lightning on the narrow path when something unthinkable happened. Lightning stepped on a rock, lost his footing and then his balance, and fell slowly to the ground. I went flying forward and tried to stop my body's forward motion by gripping the saddle and the reins tighter, but Mustafa's and my body weight was no match for the force that pulled us down. I saw the ground approaching fast and knew that this would hurt. I hoped that Lightning would be all right. We all landed on the ground and, after Mustafa and I got up, I saw blood gushing from Lightning's leg. I was shocked. I felt bad that Lightning was hurt and I knew I would have to explain this to Hasan aga. I took my shirt off and cleaned the wound as much as possible. Then we slowly walked to the village. When we arrived at Hasan aga's gate, I handed the reins to Mustafa, went to the house, and knocked on the door. Hasan aga appeared at the door.

"I need to tell you that something happened to Lightning," I said hastily. "We have fallen and he got hurt. I am sorry, Hasan aga." He looked at me with a serious expression on his face.

"Where was the wound?" he asked.

I pointed it out to him and he then exited and walked toward the yard where Mustafa was holding Lightning. He looked at the wound for a few minutes with a stern expression on his face, while I got more uneasy and nervous. Then he turned toward us.

"You go home. I will treat him. I have a medicine for his wound and he will be fine." I was relieved to hear that and we slowly headed home.

*   *   *

When not riding or star-gazing, Mustafa and I spent much of our free time exploring the hills surrounding our village. Like many teens, we sought places where we could escape adult supervision.

One time I got trapped inside a cave near the Arda River, on the opposite bank from the village of Ada, only downstream. We had ridden Lightning down a dirt road that ran downstream on Ada's bank and had crossed the river in a shallow place. It was a short ride from the river to the caves. Mustafa and I had come several times to this cave to explore it, but this time when I was walking on one of the big stones, I slipped and fell into a crack between the stone and the wall of the cave. The crack was wide enough for a person to fall into, but the bottom part narrowed like a funnel. My desperate attempts to free myself were counterproductive; the harder I tried to free myself, the deeper my body sank. Mustafa tried to help. He held my hands and pulled, but I couldn't be freed. Then he wrapped his arms and hands around the upper part of my torso and pulled hard again and again, but all to no avail. Then he decided to go to the nearest village and get help. I told him to hurry because I was in pain. He had to take the only flashlight we had, so I was trapped in the cave by myself in the pitch darkness. The pain in my back and legs was excruciating, I was trapped like wild animal. I felt like screaming and wailing as my energy decreased rapidly. I could only groan. I don't know how long I was there; I lost track of time. I don't know whether I was conscious all the time. All this was a nasty nightmare without end.

After a while, I wondered whether this was real or a dream. It must be a dream, I told myself, I couldn't be trapped. All this was stupid, I thought. When the people of our village found out I was trapped here, they would laugh at me, I knew. After what felt like an eternity, I heard steps in the distance. Then I heard Mustafa calling for me.

"Osman! Osman! Help was on the way!" he called. This phrase was music to my ears.

Chapter 4

Early in the summer of 1984 I was invited to a wedding ceremony in Ada, the Turkish name of a big village not far from my own, situated close to the banks of the Arda and Krumovitsa rivers. Potochnitsa was its official Bulgarian name. One of the graduates of my high school was getting married, and a short time after the wedding he was scheduled to begin his compulsory military service.

Weddings of Turks in rural Bulgaria usually took two days. First there was henna night, celebrated in both the bride's and bridegroom's homes. Henna night was usually held on Saturday night when the young women beautified themselves by putting henna, a brownish-red dye, on their hands. The young women, who were relatives and neighbors invited to the wedding, all gathered in a room of the house of the bride or a neighbor's house where they sang songs and danced late into the night. Before they went to bed they mixed henna with water and applied it to their fingers and in circles inside their hands, and then they wrapped their hands with pieces of cloth so the henna stayed on their hands to penetrate and pigment their skin. In the morning, they unwrapped the pieces of cloth and washed their hands — the henna had turned their hands a beautiful reddish brown in the pattern they drew, in a way, like an impermanent tattoo.

I liked the henna nights. The young men came together and danced the hora and belly dance. Mustafa and I, and other friends and peers from Ada, would come together and one of the guys who was a close relative to the wedding party would sneak a bottle of rakia, a popular alcoholic beverage in Bulgaria. We would drink the rakia, hidden from the adults in the backyard.

The next day, Sunday, was usually the wedding celebration, when the wedding guests from the bridegroom's village walked to the bride's village if the distance allowed it. The wedding celebration procession was led by musicians, usually four gypsies walking in the front, and the people followed. When the group arrived in the bride's village, they were greeted by men standing in a single line and then they were treated to a meal. Then the bride, dressed in a white bridal gown, was taken out of her parents' house and, together, bride and bridegroom in the front of the procession, walked back to the bridegroom's village.

A couple of weeks before this celebration, the couple would have been quietly married by an imam, a priest, in the village mosque. Communist authorities didn't object to this ceremony before the name change campaign happened.

In old times, when I was young, I remember the bride being veiled with a silk veil that was part of her dress, and she would be put on a horse led by the bridegroom. Gradually, more and more weddings were held with unveiled brides in white dresses. The bridegroom would be dressed in a black suit, white shirt, and tie. Most of the weddings were held in the spring, summer, and fall, since the weather was nice and permitted festivities to be performed outside.

I always thought the hora dance was a celebration of the never-ending circle of life. The music for the dancers was performed by a Turkish-speaking Roma band of a drummer, a clarinetist, an accordionist, and sometimes a saxophone player. The music the band performed was popular Turkish folk songs with names like "Karakasli yar" and "Yuksek yuksek tepelere." Kasap oyun havasi was one of the hora dances performed by the Turks living in the Rhodope Mountains.

My memories from those times are preserved like old black-and-white documentaries of a faraway time and place. I will always remember those magical nights when we gathered and danced in the warm summer air. The beauty of the hora danced in the flickering light of a fire was difficult to describe with simple words. The young people turned in circles holding each other's hands, repeating the same movements again and again. The rhythmic movement of their bodies looked like a sculpture in motion. It was an ethereal, magical moment. When one participated in the hora, one was energized by the happy mood of all participants, but it was also beautiful to watch the boys and girls dance in one big circle. There was something hypnotic in the rhythmic, repetitive movement. It made one feel not only good, but stronger as well; one wanted to go on and on. When the men danced another version of the hora, they started slowly at the beginning and then the rhythm increased and they sped up, until they started moving in a circle back and forth very fast and in a forceful way. I used to observe the hora late in night around fires or the dim light of a single light bulb and it looked as though the participants were in a trance, moving around and around.

It was a magical henna night like this when I met Leyla. Her slender body was dressed in a long red dress and she had a white scarf tied loosely around her neck. Her lovely face was framed with long black hair, and she looked enchanting as she talked and laughed with her girlfriends. When I looked at her, I thought she was ethereal. Once I saw her, I could not stop watching, my eyes constantly pulled in her direction. Her face glowed in the fire light making her beauty radiate. My heart fluttered with a new beat, the beat of attraction toward this girl, and a beat of love.

I waited for her to join the hora and then without too much hesitation, I broke into the line next to her. Her hand was soft and pleasantly warm, and she smelled like a spring bloom. I felt renewed with high energy by being so close and touching this beautiful girl. I thought that she might like me, too, because she would glance at me out of the corner of her eye and a gentle blush would spread across her cheeks. I felt something click between us, something which would grow even deeper in the weeks to come, as I looked into her soft brown eyes. Although I thought there was a spark of interest I saw there, the alarm bell of doubt rang loudly inside me. I was so intimidated by her beauty that I thought she would never pay attention to somebody like me, but nevertheless, I had to try. I didn't know if an opportunity to see her would present itself again, so it was now or never.

While we were dancing, I whispered in her ear that I would like to have a few words with her after the dance. She nodded and shyly said she wouldn't mind. I was filled with hope and desire to have time alone with her and get to know her better. My spirits and heart were flying high that night. I was enchanted by the prettiest girl of henna night.

After the dance, I told her that my name was Osman and that I was a student at Krumovgrad high school.

"I know, my cousin told me," she said quietly. "My name was Leyla and I study at the high school in Haskovo."

"You have gone far away to study," I said, with curiosity in my voice.

"My parents and my aunt arranged for me to stay with my aunt there," she replied. "The school there was very good. Of course, I come back to Ada for most of the weekends and all my vacations. There was no better place than our home in Ada," Leyla said, with sincerity in her voice. "I am helping my parents with the tobacco and the animals." She slowly lifted her gaze. I wanted her to keep looking at me, so beautiful were her eyes.

"I have been working in the tobacco field all summer, too," I said, trying not to break eye contact. I swallowed hard.

"My parents will be gone visiting relatives next week and I will be going to Krumovgrad bazaar Friday to get groceries," said Leyla and lowered her gaze.

"What a pleasant coincidence!" I said. "I will be going there, too. Maybe we can meet there and talk?" I had not really planned to go, but the presence of Leyla was enough reason and since Friday was my day off from working in the tobacco fields, I could do anything I wanted.

"How about if we meet in the morning at the marketplace?" I asked hesitantly, and looked at Leyla with hope for a positive reply.

She looked at me with her delicate eyes for a few moments and calmly said, "I think that would be possible." Then she smiled at me.

Inside I was elated. I felt like jumping and dancing, but externally I kept my cool.

For the rest of the night I observed Leyla from a distance. I could not get enough of her. The lovely Leyla was laughing and having a good time with her girlfriends, watching the dancers in the village center where the musicians were playing.

Chapter 5

All that next week I worked in the tobacco field and dreamed about Leyla, thinking about what it would be like to meet and talk to her. Finally, the long-anticipated Friday arrived, and I headed for Krumovgrad. I arrived in the town bus station with the first bus.

The station was a big, uneven asphalted square with a few, mostly old, Bulgarian-made Chavdar buses parked nearby. The building was a single-story rectangle with a metal roof and thin wood walls where the government-owned company sold tickets through a single, small ticket window, even though there were three ticket windows available — two on an internal wall and one on the opposite side of the same wall. On busy Fridays, people traveling in and out of town had to wait in long lines because there was only one open ticket window for every destination. After a while, when the patience of the people wore thin, they started pushing and shoving each other. Occasional protests in the form of desperate shouts of "Don't push!" or "Don't shove!" came from people trapped at the beginning or middle of the line. For unexplained reasons, sometimes workers would start selling tickets at one window and when the line of people moved to that window, they would shut the window and open the first window, which caused people to move in a mad, wild dash. As the day advanced and heat in the metal-roofed building became unbearable, the shouts became more desperate and tempers flared, much like a crescendo in music. After some years, two lines were put together with long metal dividers, but that didn't help much because people still pushed and shoved to get to the ticket window sooner and some people would cut in line by walking under the dividers. There were no fans to cool the air, either, as air conditioning was an unknown concept. If you had tried to explain to somebody from the bus station that there was a machine somewhere in the world that cooled the air, he would not believe you. People went through this ticket-buying nightmare every Friday. And if things were bad on Fridays, they would get even worse during traditional autumn panair, the fair. People who lived close to town preferred to travel by mule, horse, or, the cheapest and most popular, donkey. Many people simply walked.

Getting bus tickets was not the only problem people had in their attempt to get simple necessities like bread. There were two stores in town that sold bread, but that didn't mean you could find bread any time you needed it. You had a slim chance of getting bread in the late afternoon, because it was often sold out about noon, and of course, you had to wait in line and consider yourself lucky if you could buy more than two or three loaves at a time. There were often limits of how many you could purchase, and rationing most of the time. People who lived in the villages baked their own bread with flour they bought in bulk in twenty- or thirty-kilogram bags.

The same was so for yogurt. Another store sold only yogurt and milk in jars. The store was supplied with yogurt and milk in the morning and usually there was a line of people waiting before the store opened for business. Sometimes, if you were fortunate, you could buy yogurt at 3 o'clock in the afternoon but rarely. Most people living in the villages had cows and made their own yogurt just as they made their own bread. My mother made yogurt in a medium-sized copper bucket which she managed to fit into our small fridge.

There was a store that sold fruits and vegetables, but the shelves were empty most of the time. Meat was a luxury you would get only once in a while. If you just walked in and bought it, you would consider yourself lucky. If you were connected with the people who worked in the meat-selling store, you had a pretty good chance of getting some, but of course you had to return the favor with something they needed. For some reason, I always thought the situation was better in the bigger and more centrally located towns of Bulgaria, but later I found out that the situation was similar if not worse. At least the people living in the villages had a few farm animals like cows, sheep, goats, and chickens to supply them with meat and eggs.

Krumovgrad was a small town of around six thousand inhabitants. I spent two years studying there. By that time I knew the town pretty well. There was not that much to see and most of the places of interest like small stores, as well as the administrative buildings, were located in the town's center. The center was a wide square area covered with gray, square cobblestones. When you came from the marketplace, the square was a short walk. On the left side was a big gray building. The first floor of this building was a movie theatre used for concerts and occasional theater performances. The second and third floor housed the only hotel in the town. Attached to the movie theater was a restaurant called Bulgaria. Every year, in front of the movie theater on the sidewalk, a temporary platform was built during the May Day parade called manifestation to show the "ecstatic" support of the working populace for the ruling Bulgarian Communist Party. Working people, platoons of soldiers, and students from all school levels, even kindergarten, were obliged to march in groups in front of the platform where the town's secretary of the Communist party stood with a few other bureaucrats and the commander of the military garrison. The marchers were told to use their hands and flowers to wave at the party leaders. Many were made to carry big pictures of the general secretaries of the Bulgarian Communist Party and the Union of Soviet Socialist Republics, red flags and Bulgarian flags. Big pictures of Marx, Engels, and Lenin were always carried, along with slogans like "Long live BCP" and "USSR Friendship" and many others. Even though the event was supposed to be a spontaneous burst of popular support for the rulers, everybody knew that these parades were compulsory — if you failed to attend there were consequences like disciplinary punishment, and expulsion from work or school. God forbid if you were singled out as a troublemaker, an anti-regime element. Then you and your family were subjected to harassment and often ended up in prison or forcefully relocated to a different part of the country.

The town center was surrounded by other gray buildings like the movie theatre, gray being the color of choice for the socialist builders. One of the buildings situated on the south was the Savet, where the registers were kept. Here they issued new passports; every person at age 16 and older was required to have a personal passport. Wedding ceremony applications had to go through this building and receive an official government-issued marriage certificate in order to be legal. We all were so used to living this life of shortages and socialist organization that it seemed normal. We could not compare our lifestyles with the lives of the people living outside the Iron Curtain. We thought that everyone lived the way we did.

*   *   *

The bazaar where I was to be meeting Leyla was close to the bus station. I walked fast with happy anticipation. The weather was nice, warm, but not hot yet as it was about 9:30 in the morning. I walked across the road connecting the bus station with the market place and looked for Leyla, but I didn't see her. She was probably there somewhere in town, in one of the grocery stores or browsing one of the other stores. I decided to enjoy a banitchka with lemonade while I waited for her. Banitchka was basically filo pastry with feta cheese in between layers, baked in the oven with oil. Sometimes I bought one, sometimes two, of this popular breakfast item, depending on how hungry I was; the individual serving was as big as an average human hand. These and other breakfast items, like the Bulgarian version of the croissant filled with marmalade, were sold in the same store as the bread. The banitchkas were usually sold out by that time of the day, but since it was market day there would be more breakfast things than usual. I walked brusquely from the marketplace to a place downtown that sold only banitchka. It was my lucky day — there was no long line and there was banitchka to eat. I ate quickly so I could get back to the marketplace and find Leyla.

The town was getting busy now with people from the surrounding villages coming to the bazaar, and mostly middle-aged and elderly men were arriving for Friday prayer in the local mosque. It was almost 10:30 as I got back to the marketplace. I still couldn't see Leyla as I approached. I looked left and right, now all stalls were full, the crowd was growing. I was walking on the uneven asphalt of the marketplace when I saw her dressed in a long colorful dress and holding an empty shopping bag in her hand. How was it possible for a girl to be so perfect? I thought, and for a moment I was rendered breathless, the feeling of attraction so strong, so deep, like nothing I experienced before. She was tall and slender, her hair black and shiny in the sun. I approached her slowly and when I got close to her she saw me and smiled. I smiled back and said "Merhaba, Leyla," hello, how are you?

"I am very well, how are you?"

I smiled and told her how happy I was to see her, and asked if she would like to go to the pastry shop. There was only one pastry shop in town, situated in a new two-story building in the town's center and just a short walk from the marketplace. The second floor of the building was called a coffee shop, where one could drink coffee while adults played cards. There was a mehana, a traditional Bulgarian pub, in the basement, where adults went to eat and drink alcohol. The town center was V-shaped. Walking from the marketplace to the pastry shop, one passed on the left the movie theatre, and on the right, two gray buildings with apartments with a few small shops on the first floor. All the stores were government-owned. There was a small bookstore, the only one in the town. There was also a toy store, where during my childhood I had looked at the toys in the window display while my mother and grandmother and aunt went to the fabric shop next door. My aunt had a nice hand-run Singer sewing machine on which she sewed shalwars and shirts for my mother and grandmother.

There was a nice rectangular flowerbed smack in the middle of the town's center with a fountain displaying a sculpture of a completely naked woman in the middle of it; she looked as if she were a taking bath in the town center. This was the Communist party's idea of high aesthetics, a "gift" to the locals. The pastry shop was elevated above street level with a terrace-like area in the front for tables in the warm months of the year. We got to the pastry shop and decided to sit inside, next to big windows facing the town center so we could see people walking back and forth. The weather was nice, sunny and warm. It would be another hot, dry summer day. We sat next to each other and I looked at Leyla's face. I had a difficult time believing that we were sitting together. She was perfect in every way.

"It looks like it will be sunny and warm for the Friday shoppers," I said to start the conversation.

"I hope it will not be too hot," said Leyla, smiling. For a while we looked through the big window, observing the growing crowd. This pastry shop was an important place for townspeople and all guests and visitors to sit and socialize. Usually it got very crowded on Fridays. It was popular with both the young and old, non-alcohol-drinking populace because youth under the age of 18 were not served alcohol in restaurants. There were a few mothers with babies in strollers, too.

"How was your summer? How are you spending your time?" I asked Leyla, looking into her deep brown eyes.

"Most of my days are busy helping my parents with the tobacco fields," she said. "Sometimes in the evenings I have a little time to read books, or I meet with my girlfriends."

"May I ask what you talk about?" I asked.

"We talk about what we will do after we graduate from high school. Many of my girlfriends want to get married and settle down." She was serious now.

"What would you like to do after graduation?" I asked with curiosity. She thought for a moment and looked at me.

"I would like to go to nursing school," she said, "to be a nurse in a children's hospital. I think that I can do it because my grades are very good. How are your grades in school?"

"Probably not as good as yours," I responded.

"Osman, what will you do after graduating from high school?" I had been expecting this question.

"I have dreams to continue my education, too. I like animals and I would like to go to veterinary school."

Leyla smiled and said, "That was so nice, I like animals, too."

Then I came up with an idea.

"Our neighbor Hasan aga has a nice horse he lets me ride whenever I want to. Would you like to see it and have a ride?"

"Yes, I would love to see it, but I am not sure about riding it," she replied.

It was my turn to smile.

"Come on, don't be a chicken, it was fun to ride a horse."

"I am not a chicken, but I have never ridden a horse," she said defensively.

"Have you ridden a donkey?" I asked.

"Yes," she said, laughing.

"It was like riding a donkey, but you sit higher. Horses have larger backs, and can run very fast. You can get used to riding a horse. It was much more fun than riding a donkey. I love it. It was an exhilarating and liberating experience for me."

I wanted to play this small mind game with her and accuse her of being chicken, so I asked her again, "Would you like to take a ride on a horse with me tomorrow?"

She looked at me and said, "Maybe a short distance and only if you lead it."

"Then it was a deal. When and where shall we meet?" I asked eagerly.

"How about tomorrow, about 5 in the afternoon, and we can meet by the big water fountain south of the village."

Inside I felt like dancing an indecent belly dance. I was trying not to show my excitement.

"That was perfect, let's do it tomorrow. I will meet you there with Lightning," I said.

We talked for a little while, then Leyla thought that we should go our own separate ways so people from our villages didn't see us and start talking about us. I agreed, even though I felt I could spend eternity with Leyla without ever getting tired of being with her.

Chapter 6

As always, I helped my parents in the tobacco field. We didn't have much mechanization to aid us with collecting the tobacco and transporting it to our homes. Early in the spring after we got the seeds from the cooperative, we planted them in small hothouses close to the village. Later, when the young plants were big enough, we transplanted them into the fields by hand. The fields were plowed by tractors owned by cooperatives administered by the government. For transportation of the tobacco from the field to our house we used our mule or the donkey. Mules and hinnies were used for bigger loads. Few people had horses and fewer still would use them in the fields because they were prized animals; horses were used mainly as personal transportation. Everybody working tobacco was part of a cooperative. The only benefit we got from being in the cooperative was that cooperative workers would plow the fields with tractors before we planted the tobacco, and they provided and ran mobile water pumps. All this help didn't come for free; we had to pay for it — up to 50 percent of our earnings and after paying the taxes automatically deducted from our pay. As a result, we ended up with meager earnings. Thus personal transportation was mainly limited to donkeys, mules and the very few horses.

Two families, however, were able to purchase personal Soviet-made automobiles, one a ZAZ Zaporozhets and the other a Moskvich. The Zaporozhets was boxy and small with seating for four people. The engine, installed in the back of the automobile, was air-cooled by two air intake holes on the side. This must have been the noisiest car in the history of car-making because we were able to hear the car from at least a kilometer away, if not more. The locals often would say, "Roars like a bear, moves like a bug." The Voice of the Soviet Union comes to mind as a good name for the car's noise. Also, this probably was the most repaired car in the history of car-making because it broke down constantly and often had to be put on four logs during the fixing process. It was also notoriously difficult to start. Very often the help of three or four adults was required to push the car to get it going. They had to push the car so often that some of the adults would sarcastically note they developed bigger muscles in the process of pushing the venerable ZAZ. I had the opportunity to get a ride in it a couple of times, whenever the owner was able to start it. I noticed a hole in the bottom, from rust, and every time I got into the car it seemed that the hole was growing in size. The last time I got in the car the hole was so big I was afraid that my foot would go through or the seat would collapse onto the ground. The Moskvich was not any better than Zaporozhets, just bigger in size and uglier in looks. In their anger at their cars, the owners of the automobiles cursed so badly with such foul language that the neighbors advised their children not to go near when the cars were being fixed.

One wondered which were noisier, the Soviet-made cars or the tanks, which were not any more reliable than the cars. In high school we had a class called military instruction, where the instructor, an officer from the local military garrison, said it was expected that during eventual war with NATO a high percent, something like more than 40 percent, of the machinery would break down, but they had so many of them they expected to be victorious anyway. I remember one year they were driving a T-34 tank, one which I believe was built during World War II, in the streets of Krumovgrad; they were going to a parade. One of the tracks of the tank broke, and the tank lost control, hit a big tree, broke the tree in half, and came to a halt on the top of it. If there hadn't been a tree in the way, the tank would have hit and destroyed a house nearby. People were astounded that something like that could happen in this sleepy town.

*   *   *

I had not forgotten the day I would meet Leyla by the water fountain on the edge of Ada, Leyla's village, which was not too far, especially if you rode a stallion. That afternoon I washed up and told my mom that I would be riding Lightning. She told me not to be out late. I went to Hasan aga's barn, built with the same large stone blocks which were used in building our house. I had been working with Lightning on and off during the summer. Hasan aga had trained the stallion well, but I liked to work and train Lightning, too. I had slowly built a trusting relationship with this horse over time. It took lots of patience and hard work to train a horse well. Sometimes I worked in Hasan aga's yard, but I preferred to ride him on the plateau by the village, not far from Hasan aga's house. When I rode him there it felt like more than just riding; I became one with Lightning and together we became one with the mountain.

I rode Lightning fast in anticipation of seeing Leyla. Most of the ride was downslope, since Ada was lower in elevation, situated on a slight rise from the Arda River. The path was narrow, gravel-covered and winding, wide enough only for one truck or cart pulled by donkey to pass. People would usually yield to each other in wider sections of the gravel road. The road close to Ada got wider and less steep. I made it to the fountain a little bit early, but Leyla was already there, as if to get water from the water fountain. She was lovely as ever. I thought that her beauty was timeless, like a picture of a beautiful flower, that she would be forever young and never change. When I came close, Leyla saw us and got up as I got off Lightning, walked over to her, and asked how she was.

"I am fine, how are you?" she replied, beaming.

"I am fantastic," I replied. "I am always happy when I am with Lightning."

She looked with curiosity at the horse, smiled and said, "Your horse was beautiful."

"He was not mine," I admitted. "He belongs to our neighbor Hasan aga, but I am allowed to ride him whenever I want." I held Lightningby the reins.

"He was awfully big," Leyla said, looking at Lightning.

"He was big and very strong, but he was well trained and gentle. Come and touch him." I started to caress Lightning's head, neck and shoulders, to show Leyla how. "Come close, he will not harm you." Leyla was not

42

sure in the beginning. She slowly approached, put her hand on Lightning's neck and started petting him, but at that moment Lightning shook his head, which scared her. She withdrew her hand quickly and moved closer to me.

"Here, let me guide your hand," I said. I put my left hand on Lightning's bridle and gently took Leyla's hand with my right. Her hand was soft and the skin on her arm was, too. I guided Leyla's hand to Lightning's neck and this time he didn't move. "See, it was not that bad, he won't harm you."

We petted Lightning together, then I got on Lightning and, extended my hand to help Leyla get on the horse. We headed toward Arda River, which was not far from the water fountain where we'd met. By the river, between the riverbank and a tobacco field, there was a path for the mule- and donkey-drawn carts of the villagers. The fields are on a level even with the Arda valley. At that time of the day there were no people in the field, as collecting the tobacco was usually done in the morning and tobacco leaves were strung up to dry in the afternoon. Sometimes that work continued until late in the night. Stringing tobacco was arduous and dirty work, one that required the patience of a saint to string every one or only a few leaves at a time.

In the warm summer afternoon the tobacco fields looked abandoned. On one side of the narrow dirt road were lush green fields and on the other side, the sparkling emerald waters of the Arda. Here in the valley, the tobacco fields were long, kilometers in length, the edges on the banks of the river and the fields gently sloping all the way to the steep slopes of the mountainside. The high, mostly green, hills caressed the sky gently. It was so peaceful; we were so peaceful. It felt that time had stopped, time and space merged, and we were in this safe, beautiful, happy bubble, meant to be together forever in this three-dimensional picture. I wanted that day to continue forever. I was with the girl I loved and we were the center of the universe.

At that moment I told Leyla, "Hold on to me tight, now we will go fast." When Leyla's arms tightened around me, I knew we were ready to gallop. I spurred Lightning and yelled "Go, Lightning, go!" He was just waiting for the command and took off with all his might. The field and river zipped by us as we flew over the road. Finally, as we approached the end of the field and the dirt path turned away from the riverbank, I slowed down and stopped Lightning. There was a grassy area by the path on the riverbank, and I thought it was a nice secluded spot where we could sit and spend some time together.

We sat on the grass, looking at one of the many lakes of emerald green water from the Arda. We were quiet until Leyla broke the silence, worry evident on her face as she brought up the threat of the Bulgarian Communist Party name change campaign.

"Do you think that they will change our names? What do you think will happen to us?" she asked. I looked at her serious face.

"I don't exactly know, but it seems to me they will change all of our names," I said. "It seems inevitable after what I heard from my father."

"Osman, I am worried," she said.

"Don't worry," I assured her. "Whatever was meant to happen will happen, and it will happen to all of us." I tried to sound mature and wise and I thought I had heard this phrase from the elders. Despite the fear of the name change campaign, I still felt happy because I was with Leyla.

With the love I felt toward her, I was given extra courage and strength. I thought nothing could harm her or me, or even our families.

Chapter 7

Work in the field had been slowing down. We had collected most of the tobacco from the fields and now I could relax for a few days before school began. I had not been to Krumovgrad for a few Fridays. I had been busy working in the tobacco fields with my parents, with occasional breaks to go to swim in the river with Mustafa. Sometimes I stayed home on Friday to read books I enjoyed, mainly by the few foreign writers published in Bulgaria; I wanted to learn through these books about the vast world beyond the borders of Bulgaria.

Krumovgrad was exciting, a great learning experience for me. There I had the chance to experience Bulgarian culture firsthand while I was attending school. I rented a room from a Bulgarian family whose house was located far up the side of the steep hill, not far from the gymnasia, the high school, which consisted of two gray buildings. One was the school, the smaller one was the gym.

There was a nice view toward the town. Most of the houses were small or medium size with red-tiled roofs. From my room I could see the round cupolas of the Orthodox Christian Church on one side of the town center and on the other, the red-tiled roof and minaret of the big mosque where my father prayed every Friday noon. I had been studying in the school for two years; it was my third and final year. I had dreams to continue my education in veterinary school. I liked to study, but mostly I liked to read books and learn about the world. To me, it was a fascinating world we lived in; the more I learned the more I wanted to know and experience. I dreamed of traveling far away and coming back to share my adventures with my friends.

Mustafa and I went to Krumovgrad for the Friday market while the elders went to Friday noon prayers, called Jummah prayers, in the big mosque. My father would have liked me to go to the mosque with him, but he was intimidated by the authorities. Once I overheard my father and Hasan aga talking behind the fence built with thorn bushes. My father said that he would have liked me to be educated in Quranic ways, but he was afraid that I would end up like a few youths who prayed every day in the big mosque. One day they just disappeared, and later we heard they all were sent to prison just because they practiced their faith every day.

My father left for Krumovgrad early on the 7 o'clock morning bus, saying he wanted to have more time to see the market; Mustafa and I planned to catch the 9 o'clock bus, but we would still have plenty of time to see the market.

I enjoyed Mustafa's company because we were the same age, and we both enjoyed fishing and swimming in the river together. In the small meadow behind the village near the big water fountain. we also played çelik, a game that resembles baseball except it was played with a stick instead of a ball and has different rules, also called çelik çomak in other parts of the Turkish-speaking world.

Mustafa was a popular guy in the village. When the village road leading to Ada or the Krumovgrad road was washed out by rain, Mustafa would be the first to volunteer, and with a smile. Whenever neighbors' sheep or donkeys didn't come back from the mountains, Mustafa was also the first to volunteer to find them.

*   *   *

A long time ago when Mustafa and I were five or six years old the yumurtaci, the egg man, came to our village with a big mule loaded with oil, sugar, candies, and cloth for women to make clothes. He would trade his goods for eggs. Usually my mother would give me one egg so I could get seven candies. However, one day my mother said that we didn't have any eggs left because she had made börek with the eggs. I was devastated — we got a visit from the yumurtaci only once every two or three weeks, and this was my only chance to get candies. I went crying to the meydan, the village center. Then Mustafa noticed me and came over to me and asked, "Osman, what happened, why are you crying?"

Between sobs and wiping my nose on my sleeve I said, "We don't have eggs to get candies from the yumurtaci."

"Kardeş, brother, don't worry, we have plenty of eggs in our barn in the hay, so let's go and get some," Mustafa said, with determination in his voice. I followed him slowly, suddenly hopeful that I would get the desired candies. We went to the barn and in one of the nests found two eggs. Mustafa turned, smiling toward me and said, "One for you, one for me."

My mood brightened like the sun shining between the clouds after heavy rain. I returned his smile, said, "Thanks, kardeş," and we each got seven candies. After getting the candies into my pockets I forgot that I had been crying, I was the happiest kid. We of course ate the candies that day. Life was so simple that it took very little to brighten my day.

Very often I would be invited by Mustafa's parents to eat with them, and Mustafa would also come and eat with my family, so we would eat together. My mother always asked us whether we were hungry.

"You two are probably hungry after playing all day long," she would say with a smile.

I liked to tell Mustafa about what I learned at school, mostly about the things I learned from books. Mustafa's parents didn't send him to study after eighth grade because his father thought that he could use Mustafa's help around the house all year long. Mustafa would be a tobacco worker like his father — why would he need to study? To collect and process tobacco, you didn't need an education, Mustafa's father would say, you needed to work.

*   *   *

Our plan for that Friday was simple — first we would to go to the market, and after that catch the afternoon show of the new American movie we had heard good things about, *Star Wars*. I enjoyed the few American and western European, mainly French and Italian, movies shown at the local movie theater. American movies were a glimpse at a different world, a world which was developed, modern and definitely way ahead of us in technology and most areas of life. Of course, I did not verbalize my opinion in front of my teachers in high school, because I would have been put on the blacklist and become a victim of lengthy harassment if I dared say such things.

Mustafa and I talked during the long walk from our village to the bus stop not far from the riverbank. There was a small water fountain by the bus stop and we stood next to it and waited, drinking water as we went over our plans for our visit to town. There was good water flow from the fountain; somebody took care that the pipe was clean of duckweed. The fountain reservoir was uphill and used gravity to run. This fountain was always running. The amount of water decreased substantially in summer, but never stopped. We were impatiently waiting and glancing every few minutes at the road, which curved around a hill. As usual, the bus was late; it was more than twenty minutes before we saw it appear, but we were relieved; twenty minutes late was not that bad. The road to the kasaba, the town, was narrow and winding. The old and noisy Bulgarian-made bus, Chavdar, moved slowly on the uneven asphalt, dodging potholes and the occasional farm animal. Many of the grim-faced and serious passengers were forced to stand in the middle of the bus because all seats were taken.

Since I helped my family with tobacco harvest and processing, my father had given me spending money to go to the kasaba. We got to the kasaba with plenty of time to browse the vendors in the marketplace and check the stores in town. The bus stop was next to the fairly new market with asphalt and small green stalls where vendors could put their wares. There were many artisans who sold mainly handmade wood and metal wares, like spoon devices to make thread out of wool. In the fall, one could find wood burning stoves, horseshoes, chains, and spoons. Around noon we decided to have lunch. One of the best things about Friday market day was the food. The köfte, meatballs cooked on the open grill, were my favorite dish in kasaba. Tempted by the intoxicating smell of the köfte in the marketplace, we decided to have portions of köfte, somun, a loaf of bread, and a drink called lemonade made with artificial powder, not real lemons. Real lemons were rare and fancy; fruits like lemons, oranges, and bananas were grown in other countries to the south of us. We could see them and buy them once a year, before New Year's Eve, if we were lucky.

Our favorite place to hang out in town was the pastry shop in the center of the town not far from the movie theatre, the same one I had visited with Leyla. Mustafa and I headed there. On the way to the coffee shop we met up with Rafet mualim, a teacher at the local high school. He was in his 30s, and he seemed old and very mature compared with us. He considered himself an intellectual and thought himself superior to the local tobacco-working population. Even though he was an ethnic Turk like Mustafa and me, he always spoke in Bulgarian with everyone, even before 1984 and even with his fellow Turks. Like most educators during the Communist era, he thought he could express himself better in Bulgarian.

All students in all levels of education were taught, too, that the Bulgarian socialist society was superior to the capitalist Turkish society. In history class, the old Ottoman Empire was considered the root of all evil; the school curriculum portrayed Turkey as a backward and poverty-ridden capitalist society where rich people exploited the poor and the majority of people nearly starved to death. A similar story was told about

51

America, but in addition, America was described as evil, dangerous, and ready to obliterate beautiful socialist Bulgaria at any moment with its Fourth Fleet moving back and forth between the Mediterranean Sea and the Black Sea.

During this time, late in the fall, all the villages located to the south and east of Krumovgrad had been "revived," as the Communist rulers described the name change campaign. Ethnic Turkish villagers had been forced at gunpoint to change their Turkish names to Bulgarian. Witnessing these events in the summer of 1984, Rafet underwent a dramatic change in his thinking. He could not understand why the Bulgarian government was using force in the name change campaign. He was disgusted by the brutality of the regime against peaceful, civil people. The most obvious sign of Rafet's change was that he stopped speaking Bulgarian in public and started speaking Turkish.

Rafet greeted us with a forced smile. "Hello, Osman, Mustafa," he said. I detected anxiety behind the smile.

"Hello, comrade Rafet," we said.

"Please don't call me comrade, you can call me aga," he said, with slight irritation in his voice. "Aga" was the term used by local Turks to address any male who was older than they were, an old Ottoman term passed from generation to generation to the present time.

"Could we sit in the pastry shop together?" Rafet asked. This was completely out of character for him. He was not usually known to mingle with his students, especially the ones who came from the villages where people worked at "degrading" manual labor, like growing tobacco, for a living. He came across as a high-flying intellectual or, more precisely, as a snob.

"Yes, let's sit down, Rafet aga," I said.

"How was school going for you, Osman?" he asked.

"Pretty good," I said. "I am starting my last year of high school soon." I sensed tension in our small talk.

"That's good," Rafet replied, then added in a somber tone, "Unfortunately, our lives never will be the same after the Communists are done forcing name change upon the Turks."

"Why are you saying that, Rafet aga?" I asked bluntly. "I thought you believed under socialist rule our lives would get perpetually better, as we have been taught in school."

"Yes, I believed that," he said sadly, "but what was happening now was that we see the true face of Communism — violent and uncompromising. We should have seen this coming, but we were too busy with our daily lives. They changed the names of all Pomaks living in Bulgaria from Turkish-Muslim to Bulgarian Slavic in the 1970s. Next, they changed the names of all Muslim gypsies to Bulgarian. We should have known that next they would change the names of the Turks, as well."

"Wouldn't it be right to say that this was a dictatorial regime?" I said. "In the end, this name change campaign could not happen without the order of the dictator Todor Zhivkov."

"Unfortunately, you might be right" said Rafet, turning his gaze toward the square.

"Wouldn't it be right to say that the whole socialist system was wrong," I said, "because it allows one person to consolidate political power in his hands and treat people like slaves? Basically, our dictator Todor Zhivkov can decide to wipe out half of the Turkish minority in Bulgaria, and there was no force in Bulgaria to oppose him."

After short silence, Rafet, deep in thought, replied, "We have been living a lie with socialism, Communism and equality have been a lie. Our leaders live like kings, and we barely have enough to survive. We cannot criticize them because of fear of becoming pig food."

"What do you mean by 'becoming pig food'?" I asked.

"When the Communists first took over political power they imprisoned most of the opposition. Many of them were killed and their bodies were fed to the pigs," Rafet said, watching to see our reaction.

Suddenly, at that moment, from the public address system, booming like loud thunder, came the announcement that a member of Politburo of the Central Committee of the Bulgarian Communist Party was speaking at the local Communist meeting and his speech was to be broadcast over the PA. The voice of the party leader thundered like the voice of a god, loud and omnipotent. It could be heard throughout the town:

"Comrades, we are in an era of great change. A great part of our nation that was converted to Islam under the Ottoman yoke has returned to our common Bulgarian family. Our blood brothers and sisters, whose national self-identity was suppressed for centuries by foreign enslavers, have returned to our family. Now Bulgaria was a single-nationality state, which includes no parts of other peoples or nationalities. The Bulgarian citizens from Islamic faith are descendants of Bulgarians. No emigration to Turkey will be allowed. All who are dancing to the tune of Ankara's propaganda and their nationalist agents will be able to move, not to Turkey, but to another area of Bulgaria, like the Belene concentration camp, where they

might find permanent residence. We have the means to defend ourselves from the internal enemy; we have the dictatorship of the proletariat. Any resistance will be crushed with an iron fist."

We sat in stunned silence for several minutes.

"I cannot believe this nonsense," Rafet said with disdain. "This was outrageous. Sooner or later their brutal campaign will fail." He rose in disgust. "We have heard enough lies and nonsense for the day," he said, storming away in disgust. "I will see you boys later." It would be many years before I saw him again. We too left after a few minutes and waited downtown until the afternoon showing of *Star Wars*. The fear that our names would be changed hung over our heads like the sword of Damocles.

It was a short walk from the pastry shop to the movie theatre, the place I liked the most in this sleepy town because I could glimpse a world I couldn't dream of physically visiting. The movies made me yearn to visit faraway places, making me happy, taking my attention from the gray and drab reality of our advanced socialism, from the endless routine of working in the tobacco fields, from the advancing line of the name change campaign.

The building where the movie theatre was situated was pretty big for Krumovgrad. The first floor was the lobby and movie theatre with a single screen and a capacity of about 200 people. There were also a balcony and a projection room. The spacious lobby was empty of furniture; there were no chairs for people waiting to see the movies. Crowds gathered in small groups and talked loudly. Most of the visitors to the movies were youngsters like Mustafa and me. We had to deal with the unavoidable line for tickets. I volunteered to buy tickets and stoically waited at the end of a long line. *Star Wars* was popular with the local youth; we didn't get movies like this every day. If the line at the bus station was bad, this one was worse because the youth here were feisty. After inevitable pushing and shoving back and forth, I got the coveted tickets. We had a few minutes to look at the posters with the names and pictures of the next movies coming to town.

"Are they good or are they Soviet?" I verbalized my thought, to which Mustafa smiled a wide smile.

"Too bad, they are Soviet," Mustafa said.

"Guess who is not going to those movies?" I asked, even though there was no need.

"I guess you and I," said Mustafa, still grinning.

Visiting the movie theatre was an even more interesting experience when there was an Indian film showing. Suddenly, along with the usual crowd of Bulgarian and Turkish movie-goers, there was a throng of rambunctious Gypsy visitors. They talked loudly and they were always happy that they would be seeing an Indian film. They never missed one. The young women were dressed in colorful dresses, the older ones dressed with even more colorful shalwars. They talked and laughed amongst themselves, always seeming happy and carefree, even though they were poor. Soon wearing shalwars in public would be prohibited — since there were no Turks in Bulgaria, the authorities would claim, people should not be wearing clothing associated with Ottoman Turkish garb. I heard that the shalwars of many women caught by the police were cut up with scissors in public.

Everybody enjoyed the music and dances of the Indian films, but there was a special place in the heart of the Gypsies for the Indian music, which they would record on tape and try to emulate and reproduce in their own singing. Above all, the Gypsies were the best belly dancers because they were not inhibited, they were free spirits always celebrating life.

That afternoon we saw *Star Wars*. I was excited because the small group rebels could fight a stronger evil, a well-organized power like the Empire. For the duration of the movie I forgot about the name change campaign and enjoyed the story. I thought that this was the best movie I had ever seen. We had been given a glimpse of a different world and it felt as though we were part of the action, we were there with Luke Skywalker.

Chapter 8

After the movie, I went to visit my grandparents in Kıyılar köyü, which was the Turkish name, Kamenka the Bulgarian name, of the village. Before I started school, I wanted to help them with whatever I could. It was the last weekend of my summer vacation, and soon I would not have free time. Kıyılar köyü was a small village near Krumovgrad, where my grandparents lived in a big house with a walled-in yard, built during the time of the Ottoman Empire. I knew they had a load of wood which needed to be chopped before winter. Mustafa headed home with the last bus, and I headed for Kıyılar köyü. I walked on the dusty edge of asphalt highway leading from Krumovgrad to Ivaylovgrad. Kıyılar köyü was only about one kilometer from the town. When I was very young I thought this was a very long distance. There was a narrow cobblestone main road built by the first settlers here during the years of the Ottoman Empire. Most of the houses were old.

During the long, busy summer days of my childhood, my mother took me to live with my grandparents, her parents. There was a big granary, or silo, attached to the fence and there were two barns, both connected to the wall which was itself connected to the house. The outer walls of the granary and barns created a natural fence around the house. The yard in front of the house was enclosed with a stone fence and there was a large gate right in the middle of it that opened to the narrow cobblestone road outside. A grapevine which still produced sweet grapes had been planted by my ancestors in the front of the house. My grandmother always encouraged me to eat the grapes when I came to visit. She said no one really knew when this grapevine had been planted, because no one wrote down the date, the plant was simply everlasting. It was possible it was planted when the house was built more than 200 years ago. Maybe my grandmother thought the age of the grapevine would somehow help me live a long life. It always amazed me how a plant could last that long. When I was kid I used to play in the yard. I would climb the mulberry trees and eat the big red-and-white juicy berries; I would throw a few unripe ones at the donkey in the yard, watching and giggling as the donkey moved and shook its ears.

I felt safe in my grandparents' home; it was like my second home, where I was always welcomed. Through my grandparents, I felt that I permanently resided in this village, as if I belonged there. Walking next to the fence built with big rectangular stones, warmed by the mid-September sun, I had the eerie feeling that, somehow, long ago I had been here before in another lifetime. I felt eternity playfully joking with me in its gentle embrace at that moment. I attributed the feeling to the time I had spent there during the summers, when my parents would leave me there so they could concentrate on working the tobacco.

I opened the gate, which made a familiar screeching sound that I interpreted as the old house welcoming me. I walked from the narrow stone paved road to the wide yard of my grandparents' house. There was my grandfather still dressed like an Ottoman Turk in wide black trousers, short black jacket over a white buttoned-up shirt, and a red fez around which a black scarf was tied, short white beard and round eyeglasses. He kept his old silver watch in the small pocket of his sleeveless black jacket. From time to time, he would open the old watch with the white face, very fine black Roman numerals and delicate hands, and check to see whether it was time for prayer. I will always remember him like this. Times changed, but my grandfather remained the same. There was something timeless about my grandparents and their wisdom accumulated through their long life. Most important, they had survived wars and had seen the change from a feudal empire to capitalism and fascism and later to Communist rule in Bulgaria.

When my grandfather was born, in the very house where he still lived, this land was a part of the Ottoman Empire, not Bulgaria. The house was built by my ancestors, Ottoman Turks, big and solid like the Empire at that time. The big house had outer walls more than a half-yard thick that reminded me of a medieval castle. The building of this house coincided with the birth of a great country across the Atlantic Ocean during the year 1776, the age of the house being known through the Ottoman register. It was a peaceful time in this place, the heartland of the Ottoman Empire. Most of the men from that generation were not warriors, they were administrators, builders, and merchants. In those times, many ethnic and diverse religious groups lived alongside each other in peace and harmony, engaged in peaceful work and business with each other.

For most of the year, the spacious foyer would smell of prunes because my grandmother stored and dried prunes in a big ceramic pot there. The sweet smell was like a natural air freshener, and I would always associate that scent with my grandparents' home.

Grandfather was chopping wood when I arrived.

"Selam aleyküm, Grandfather," Hello, I said, smiling, happy to see him.

"Aleyküm selam, Osman," said the old man, putting the ax down. My grandfather often greeted me with, "How are you, my ram?" Every time he saw me he called me "my ram" affectionately.

"I am fine, I am ready to chop wood, Grandpa," I said with a little exaggerated enthusiasm to show my grandfather that I meant business.

"Maşallah, God willed it, you have grown since I have seen you last time. You look like a wrestler, you should participate in the wrestling competition held during the fall." I smiled with pleasure. He liked to repeat this about wrestling almost every time we met, because he liked wrestling very much. I kept reminding him that my heart was in horse racing, not wrestling. "I will go and tell your grandmother that you are here, she will be happy to see you."

When my grandmother appeared at the door, she was all smiles and happy to see me. She walked quickly toward me and embraced me, kissing both my cheeks.

"It is so nice to see you, Osman, we haven't seen you all summer, and we missed you so much. You have grown and become stronger. Remember, you used to spend every summer here," grandmother said, smiling wide while rubbing my back and shoulders as if she was afraid I would disappear.

"How could I forget? I remember being repeatedly chased by the neighbors' ducks, I was scared to death by those ducks," I said with false indignation. This elicited hearty laughter from the beloved old couple. "This summer I have been working in the tobacco fields with my parents. I have been working for the money I will need when I go to school in the fall."

"That was great, Maşallah. You have grown, you are becoming a big, mature and a smart man."

My grandmother was dressed in a dark blue, wide shalwar and shirt made from the same material. In the cool months she wore a blue hırka, or cardigan, and a black feredje, which was a long black coat that covered her entire body except for her head. She was never seen without a white scarf covering her head. In public she would tie the scarf in front, under her chin, but in the privacy of her home she would tie the scarf on the back of her head exposing more of her face.

"You must be tired from the walk from town. Why don't you sit next to your grandfather, and I will bring you ayran, a yogurt shake, to drink."

Not wanting to offend her, I decided to sit outside, next to my grandfather on the bench that was put next to the white outer wall of the house. The September evening warmth was pleasant and a satisfying warm wind was blowing from the mountaintops surrounding the village. The setting sun's last rays hit the red roofs of the neighbors' houses and the top of the trees. It was the perfect weather for chopping wood for the coming winter.

"Grandfather, I need to tell you about what happened in town today. This big shot from Sofia came to town, a member of the Politburo, and said that that we are not Turks, but Bulgarians who were assimilated. He said that since we realized that we are Bulgarians we are voluntarily changing our names back to Bulgarian from Turkish. Are we Bulgarians who have been converted to Islam and assimilated to Turks?" My grandfather looked at me over his round eyeglasses, as if he could not believe that I was asking such a question.

"That was utter nonsense, young man," he said. "We are ethnic Turks, we are not assimilated Bulgarians. Forcing us to accept new Bulgarian names will not change the fact that we think about ourselves as ethnic Turks. I was raised a Turk, your father and you, too. Those people in the Politburo and their general secretary are a bunch of criminals for forcing people to change their names at gunpoint. " He looked in my eyes and continued. "In the faithful Muslim tradition, Ottoman Turks gave the Bulgarians the right to maintain their own national conscience, by giving them the right to study their own language and develop their own culture within the boundaries of the Ottoman Empire. The Turkish sultans followed the instructions in the Quran, to be tolerant of two older and closely related religions, Judaism and Christianity, which share with Islam the essential characteristics of belief that there is only one God.

"The Ottoman Empire was protector of the Orthodox Church and millions of Orthodox Christians," grandfather continued, "with the requirements of obedience and payment of poll tax in a time when Ottoman neighbors and many other European countries oppressed, expelled and slaughtered their minorities. The Islamic Ottoman Empire was willing to respect the difference in its subjects. Ottomans, instead of exterminating their Christian subjects, let them be."

Then my grandmother reappeared with a big round tray on which she usually served her wonderful Turkish coffee in small ceramic cups. There were three big copper cups full with ayran. She made the best Turkish coffee and ayran in the village. The three of us sat on the bench, each with a copper cup, taking big gulps of the refreshing drink. My grandmother went back inside the house and my grandfather slowly turned his head toward me with a serious expression on his face.

"Establishment of the Ottoman Empire in the Bulgarian territories," he began, "brought an end to the endless feudal wars and suffering of the Bulgarians at each other's hands, and enabled Christian Bulgarians to live in peace and prosper. They were given the right to preserve and develop their own culture, religion and language."

At that point my grandfather took off his eyeglasses and cleaned them with the handkerchief he carried in his pocket.

"Remember this," he said. "By 1490, in Catholic Spain and Portugal, the Jews who refused to accept Christianity were forced to leave Spain and Portugal or were slaughtered. The Ottoman sultan, Beyazid II, welcomed the Jews with open arms to the Ottoman Empire. Beyazid II issued a formal invitation for all the expelled Jews to come and live within the boundaries of the empire. A great number of European Jews moved to the European and Asian parts of the Ottoman Empire. They contributed to the rising power of the Empire by introducing new ideas, ways to do business, know-how and skills. Of all the minorities, the Jews were the most loyal non-Muslim subjects of the sultan. They supported the empire until the very end of its days."

I was puzzled. "If the Christian minorities were happy, how come they rebelled against the empire and established their own countries from parts of the empire?" I asked, thinking that the question was reasonable.

"No empire lasts forever," my grandfather replied sadly. "As the Ottoman power ebbed, the diversity which had been its strength in one era became its weakness in the next. Unfortunately, during the last few decades, the empire was ruled by incompetent and despotic sultans who were the reason for widespread corruption of government officials. They were unfair and abusive toward Christian minorities, which led to revolt and strife among them."

At that time my grandmother came back with her shiny old copper tray bearing three cups of black, steaming Turkish coffee. I smiled and said, "Grandmother, you make the best coffee, thank you."

"That was because I make coffee every day for us," she said, smiling back.

My grandfather took a sip of the coffee and agreed with me.

"This is good coffee, isn't it?" Then he turned toward me. "I have to tell you about my conversation with bay Radichko." "Bay" was an expression used for an older man in the Bulgarian language. Bay Radichko and Milena, his wife, were close friends with my grandparents and they were also my aunt's Bulgarian neighbors.

"A few days ago bay Radichko came to visit us here. He was very upset about the name change campaign. He said that he had been hearing these rumors about the names of the Turks to the south and east of the town being changed forcefully. He was not happy with these rumors, so he decided to investigate the truthfulness of the claims himself and went to the villages to ask the villagers. Unfortunately, his worries were confirmed. The people told him about their names being changed forcefully and of beatings and threats that were used. Then bay Radichko went straight to the party secretary in Krumovgrad to complain about this unacceptable situation. The secretary told him that decision had been made by the general secretary of the BCP to change the names of all ethnic Turks in Bulgaria. Bay Radichko insisted that this policy was wrong and should be reversed immediately, but the party secretary told him to leave his office and not return, otherwise he would contact the chief of the local police to take care of him. Furious, bay Radichko left the office. The next day he was contacted by the police chief and made to go to the police station where the police chief told him if he bothered the party secretary again he would be sent to Belene concentration camp on an island in the Danube River where arrested Turks were held.

"Bay Radichko said that he didn't agree with this policy of forceful name change campaign, but there was nothing he could do. He said that all the time he thought that he was living in a free society, but now he realized how wrong he had been."

My grandfather sighed and took another sip of his coffee, before adding, "In the end, all people are God's children and somewhere, back in time, we all have a common parent, we are all related and connected even if we deny it. Yes, we are separated by our beliefs, but we can live in peace together. Peace is essential for happiness, we are people first and believers next. Don't worry about anything, this Communist regime will collapse and this hateful name change campaign will be reversed. Most important, never ever be afraid of anything."

I did not have reason to doubt the words of my grandfather. He was known as the most reputable merchant in the kasaba region before 1945.

He used to own a big building in downtown Krumovgrad, the first floor of which was a retail store for miscellaneous groceries and other products. But when the Communists took the reins of power in 1945 thanks to invading Soviet troops, they nationalized his store and all the land he owned. He said that he was ready to fight the Communists, but my grandmother's foresight and influence upon him stopped him from grabbing a rifle — which saved his life and probably his family's lives, too. He lost pretty much everything except the house of his great-grandparents. He used to tell me about the brutality of the Communists perpetrated against all wealthy landowners and business owners. He told me about waterboarding, Communist style. If people resisted signing the papers for nationalization of their properties, the Communists would tie the person's legs and lower him, headfirst, into the well. They would keep his head in the water for a while, lift him out and ask him again whether he would sign. If he refused, they dropped him back into the water until he agreed to sign or drowned.

In grandfather's mind, Communists were up to no good. They had stolen his land and attacked his religion by saying horrible things like, "Allah doesn't exist." My grandparents embraced religion with great zeal, not because they were narrow-minded fanatics who would carry hatred toward other religions, but simply because they were brought up that way. Despite growing up in an era which was long gone and their limited use of Bulgarian, my grandparents still had many Bulgarian friends. My grandparents were educated in a religious school, where other subjects like math were studied as well as the Quran. Grandfather was even a little suspicious of all the new electric communication tools of the modern age because he had been taught in school that the Quran disapproved of pictures of humans.

From time to time my grandfather would tell me about their experiences during World War II. I was amazed my grandfather was even around at that time, and I was curious about his experiences because we had studied that war in high school. Initially, my grandparents had only heard about the war, which was fought in faraway places; it didn't affect them directly. Then one day they were stunned to find out that the local rulers of the Bulgarian Fascist regime, which was collaborating with Nazi Germany, intended not only to bring the Nazis to my grandparent's village, but to station Nazi officers on one floor of my grandparent's big house. My grandfather didn't like it, but grudgingly had to agree or face the wrath of the Bulgarian Fascist regime.

They had never seen a Nazi or even a German before, said my grandfather. They arrived in big shiny cars, motorcycles, and trucks pulling many cannons. They disembarked in the village center and all the villagers gathered to look at them. They were well dressed, well groomed, and sleek, looking fit and healthy, tall and fair-skinned; many young and handsome blond soldiers. They spoke a language the villagers could not understand, but all of them spoke and walked as if they owned the place. Those soldiers were full of themselves. Their officers walked like roosters, all puffed up. They already acted as if they owned and ruled the world. At that point, the Nazis were getting ready to invade Greece, but little did they know that Greek resistance fighters had prepared a trap for them in the narrow passage on the Greek side of the Rhodope Mountains. After the Nazis had left for Greece, we later heard they were ambushed there, and many of the soldiers and officers who had been stationed in my grandfather's village were killed.

"What business did they have, invading foreign land so far away from Germany?" my grandfather would say. "They deserved what they got there in Greece. It was somebody else's country."

When my grandmother overheard that story, she would add, "It was such a pity that all those young men had to die. I always felt sorry for their mothers, wives and families."

"The Bulgarian Fascist government sent their soldiers to Greece, too," my grandfather would continue "Most of northeastern Greece was given to Bulgaria by their Nazi masters. The Bulgarian army was quick to return in 1944 with their tails tucked in, after causing horrendous suffering to the local Greeks by starving, killing and deporting them to other parts of Greece."

Chapter 9

My grandmother was one of the most generous and selfless women in my family. She always gave priority to the welfare of her family, which included the health and well-being of her daughters, my aunts. She had three daughters — one lived in Krumovgrad with her husband, the second, my mom, lived in Çaliköy with her family, and the third one moved to Istanbul, Turkey, in 1977, during the last organized mass emigration of Turks from Bulgaria to Turkey. My grandmother would visit my aunt in Krumovgrad often, and she became friends with their Bulgarian neighbors. My grandmother's heart was as big as the universe and she loved me as if I was her own son. I visited her often whether by myself or with my mother, and she always had sweet candy, baklava or saraylı, a sweet pastry, and hoşaf, prune juice, waiting for me.

My grandmother would collect the yellow and blue plums from the orchard in big baskets. She made two or three lengthwise cuts on the fruit and set them on top of a colorful sheet to dry them outside in the sun. After the plums were dry, she would mix them with sugar in big pots and boil the mix. After the mix cooled down it was ready to drink. The thirst-quenching juice was called hoşaf.

One day, when I was seven or eight years old, I was playing in the yard of my grandparents' house when somebody knocked on the fence door. I went to the door and slowly opened it. There was an old gypsy woman standing there, stooped over, with a small thin body. She was dressed in an old, dark-colored shalwar and old black feredje that looked like a cloak. Her disheveled hair was protruding from under her small black headscarf. The skin on the back of her hands was dark and wrinkly and matched the wrinkles on her face. Her nose was big and round like an eagle's beak, her eyes were set deep in her skull like black coal. For a moment I thought that I was seeing Baba Yaga, the fearsome witch from the Russian fairy tales I used to read. Baba Yaga was known for eating small children like me. I thought she was going to strike at any moment and cut me in half with a single bite. She started to speak, but I did not wait to make sense of what she was saying. I was scared out of my pants and ran off to the safety of my grandmother's side, back in the house. We were alone at home as my grandfather had gone to the mosque for Friday prayer.

"Grandma, grandma," I shouted, struggling to take a breath. "Baba Yaga is outside!"

"Baba who? What does she want?" asked Grandma without turning toward me, busy cooking a meal.

"I don't know, I don't know," I responded hastily. "She is waiting outside."

"I will go and see what she wants," said my grandmother slowly, and I made sure that I was behind her at all times as I followed her, just in case the woman waiting outside decided to grab me.

My grandmother opened the door and looked upon the woman and smiled.

"Selamün aleyküm, Safie," Hello, Safie, said the gypsy woman.

"Aleyküm selam, Emine," Hello, Emine, my grandmother replied, while I stood in amazement at the fact that she knew Baba Yaga by name. This was not enough, though, to convince me to come out of hiding behind Grandma's big shalwar.

"Welcome, welcome," said my grandmother, and she put her hand in a most friendly manner on Emine's shoulder and invited her inside the fenced yard. I was astonished at what was happening.

"I want to do a fortune-telling for you, Safie," said the fortuneteller in a hoarse, husky voice.

"Yes, of course, you are welcome to do a reading," Grandma replied, with a gentle kind voice and a smile.

"I have an idea, though," said my grandmother. She looked at me, smiling. "Why don't you do a fortune-telling for Osman here?" And she held me by my shoulder and gave me a nudge toward the gypsy fortune teller. I pushed back, grabbing my grandmother's shalwar the way a drowning person grabs a lifeline.

We went inside the house into the room with the big open fireplace. A small fire threw a flickering light into the room. My grandmother brought three sheepskins and placed them in a circle in front of the fireplace, even though there was a divan by the wall. We sat on the floor on the sheepskins in old Turkish style.

"How do you want to read, Safie?" asked my grandmother.

"I want to read with dry beans," replied the fortune teller, and my grandmother went to the foyer to get the dry beans, leaving me alone with

72

the frightful Gypsy woman.

She sat cross-legged on one of the sheepskins facing the fireplace. My grandmother returned with a handful of dry beans on a copper plate and a big sheet, which she put on the floor between the sheepskins. She sat kneeling on her own legs, with her feet tucked under her bottom and I sat in the same way.

My grandmother gave the beans to the fortune teller, who removed all but a few from the plate, then shook it until the remaining ones fell to the sheet spread evenly on the floor between us. The gypsy stared at the beans for some time mumbling quietly to herself. After a while, she looked up at me and I quickly dropped my gaze, afraid to look her in the eye. She turned to my grandmother and said, "This was an interesting reading about your young man. I see one right path Osman can take in the future. His destiny leads him to a land far away. But he will have to go through fire and water to get there. It will be very difficult, but he can do it with the help of many different people. This path is glorious and he will be blessed with a long life, but you have to make the right choice at the crossroad. When the time comes he will know which choice is the right one for him, but it will not be an easy choice to make."

"But how can we know what you are saying in true?" asked my grandmother, smiling and turning her head toward me, as she winked. I had the feeling that she was not taking this fortune-telling business seriously at all, because even though the news was bad she kept smiling.

"It is all up to you to believe in what I said or reject it," said the fortune teller in a resigned voice. "All I am telling you is what I read from the beans. It is up to Osman to choose the path that was right for him."

After a few moments of silence, after the reading had a chance to sink in, the gypsy woman stood up and looked my grandmother in the eye and said, "Safie, it is time for me to leave." Then she unexpectedly turned toward me, which startled me and added, "But for now, my boy, you don't worry about anything. You will have many years of happiness before you come to this crossroad."

Later my grandmother gave the woman a whole loaf of bread, a big slice of feta cheese, vegetables from the garden and some old clothes. I realized then that fortune telling was the service and all the food and clothing was the payment. This was a way for the poor gypsy woman to keep her honor while she begged for charity for her family. My grandmother would let the gypsy woman in her home when most of the other people thought that gypsies were dirty and dishonest. I remember and understood the meaning of all this later when my grandmother would retell the story and laugh and tease me about how scared I was. She would always end the retelling by saying that she did not take the reading seriously.

*   *   *

During my childhood, my grandmother used to visit my aunt who lived in Krumovgrad and she liked to take me with her. The town was an interesting place for me, because there were at least two big grocery stores which used to have a lot of candy. There was also a store that sold only toys. I used like to go in and look at all the toys. No one ever bought me one, but I still enjoyed looking at the toys displayed inside. According my parents' and grandparents' philosophy of raising children, the children who invent their own toys and play with them grow to be very intelligent in adult life. I suspected, however, that their motivation and main reason not to buy me a toy was to save money. On the other hand, my grandparents did let me play with the walnuts which were stored in a big wooden barrel in the pantry. I painted them in different colors to represent different armies. I marked the ranks of officers and soldiers with dots, lines, and stars. The empty lokum, Turkish Delight, and candy boxes became tanks and trucks. I would play with the batch of walnuts from this year's crop until the time came to prepare baklava for the celebration of that year's Bayram celebration. So I would lose my beloved walnut soldiers until the next year's crop of fresh walnuts. Then my mother, aunt and grandmother would come together and go to the orchard not far from my grandparents' house and, of course, I would go along with them and help them as much as I could. They took the walnuts into the garden where they skinned the green covers and laid the walnuts out to dry. After they dried, some were put in a big wooden box in a cupboard in my grandmother's house, and another lot would be put in bags and my mother would take them to our village where they would be stored in another wood box in the cupboard. The night we collected them, I would go with excitement and shining, happy eyes. I would open the lid of the box and look at the walnuts as if they were gold treasure and I was the owner. Mustafa and I would meet at my parents' house and sort the walnuts by size. The big ones would be the generals, medium size ones the officers, and the smaller ones would be the soldiers. Then we would get our paints for school and mark the walnuts according to the sorting we had done earlier. Our happiness and excitement had no limits, nor did our imagination about the configuration of the battles. Of course, I was almost always the winning party of the battles — because I owned the walnuts I decided who would have the winning army and who would have the losing one. My mother didn't mind us playing with the walnuts either, as long we put them back in the wood box after we were finished. Some of the battles were reenactments, but most were made up battles between the Soviets and Nazis from the time of World War II. The red ones were the Soviets, the black ones were the Nazis, and the green ones were the Americans. Our battles were inspired by the many Soviet propaganda movies depicting World War II, showing how great and glorious the Soviet soldiers were. Other Soviet movies were quite dull, however.

During the visits to my aunt's home, my grandmother would enjoy visiting with her Bulgarian neighbors. My aunt used to repeat that she loved her Bulgarian neighbors who were friendly to her family and she got along with them just fine. She said that she had been living there for many years and she had not heard one single bad word from her Bulgarian neighbors. She bitterly complained, however, about her only Turkish neighbor, a lady who spread rumors that my aunt's children were sickly and predisposed to illness. My aunt was worried that people would believe these lies and that her children would have a difficult time getting married. My aunt used to repeat from time to time that we Turks were not bad people, but our trait of engaging in the spreading of rumors was bad.

While walking though the yard, if she saw the Bulgarian ladies sitting on an outside bench or working in their vegetable garden in the yard of their house, my grandmother would go up and engage them in conversation. Most of the elderly Bulgarian ladies spoke Turkish pretty well. The

Bulgarians in Krumovgrad were refugees from the region of Thrace, which now belongs to Greece. Many Bulgarians had to move from Greek Thrace to southern Bulgaria where they lived among the Turkish population.

The old Bulgarian ladies preferred to talk to my grandmother in Turkish because their Turkish was better than my grandmother's Bulgarian. My grandmother spent a lot of time sitting at an outside table with Baba Milena, the wife of Radichko. In the Bulgarian culture, all elderly women can be called "baba", grandmother, without fear of offending them. I always called Milena "baba" because I thought it was a respectful thing to do. Even though baba Milena looked ancient to me — her face was wrinkled, her skin was not firm — her body and mind were strong. She always was as kind to me as my grandmother was nice to baba Milena's grandchildren. Baba Milena had this candy dish which she would bring from inside containing a variety of exotic candies and chocolate which I loved. Her daughter, who lived in Sofia, was married to a diplomat, and she would bring baba Milena chocolates and candy from foreign countries. When baba Milena saw that I was eyeing the candy dish, she would smile and encourage me to take more. Baba Milena was retired like my grandmother and they had lots of free time, despite the fact that they both had gardens and my grandmother had a small flock of sheep. I liked to listen to the accents of the Bulgarian ladies as they spoke Turkish with my grandmother. Once baba Milena complained that their granddaughter was ill and they took her to a doctor, but the child was not improving. Grandmother immediately volunteered to pray to help heal baba Milena's granddaughter. Baba Milena and her family were like an extended family to my grandmother. My mother and aunt said a healing prayer, too, but my grandmother had time to heal because she was retired and had the time to visit Krumovgrad. So anytime the elderly Christian Bulgarian ladies complained that their grandchild was ill, my grandmother immediately volunteered a prayer. This healing prayer was recited in Arabic by a Turkish Muslim woman for a Bulgarian Christian child. I don't know how, but her prayer would work in unfathomable ways. Later the old ladies would come to my grandmother and tell her how the prayer worked for the grandchild, and soon the child was feeling fine. Later in life, I came to think that maybe the selfless love and compassion of my grandmother for all living beings somehow nurtured the sick Bulgarian and Turkish children back to health.

"All children need love," my grandmother would say. She would caress and talk to them in a soothing manner, exactly the same way she would for me when I was sick. I was often jealous of the attention my grandmother paid to other children.

I always remember those elderly ladies, sitting there, smiling at each other, and having a good time together. They were able to ignore the prejudices shown by others belonging to a certain religion or nationality. They had peace and genuinely cared for each other in their hearts.

Later, when I was in high school, I had a difficult time believing that these prayers worked because I was indoctrinated to believe only in the material world. According to the atheist, Communist schoolteachers, Allah, God, did not exist. At school, if you even suggested that you believed, you instantly became the target of lengthy harassment by teachers who would jump all over you with unrelenting Communist zeal and ask you to prove where Allah was or provide any proof of Allah's existence.

Another time I remember my grandfather telling me a story about my grandmother. In late fall, the sheep were taken for the last time up the hills to graze on the grass of eastern Rhodope Mountains by one of the village shepherds. The families in the village would take turns taking all villagers' sheep to the hills to graze. My grandmother did this many times, so she was familiar with the terrain. However, when the weather was quiet and temperate down in the valley where the village was situated, up in the mountain's northern hills it could be very windy. The cold northern wind called "poyraz" would be blowing during late fall and it could even snow. In contrast, the white wind, which tends to blow early in the spring from the south, was said to blow from North Africa and was known to melt lots of snow overnight.

When the sheep were brought back that autumn for the last time, one of my grandmother's ewes didn't come home with the flock. My worried grandmother suspected that the ewe was pregnant and now was stranded high on the mountain with a newborn lamb and could not come home. After short deliberation, and against the wishes of my grandfather, she decided to go up the mountain alone to find the ewe and bring her home. He could not go with her because he didn't feel well; it seemed, with weather turning cool, he had caught the first cold of the season. She walked fast along the narrow cobblestone road, up toward the narrow mountain road that went up and down before the climb to a high hill. Past the hill was the plateau where sheep were led to graze.

My grandmother knew there were wolves on the mountain and they would be active deep into the winter and attack the sheep in the villages at higher elevations. One winter she remembered that the local hunters killed a lone wolf and laid the body in the village meydan, or square. The size of the wolf defied imagination. She thought that people's imagination exaggerated the danger of the wolves, because she had seen them in the wild and she knew that they were shy animals. That evening when my grandmother left to look for the sheep, night fell fast as the daylight hours were getting shorter and nights longer with the onset of fall. My grandfather got really worried. He went to the neighbors and alerted them and they all came to my grandfather's place where a big fire was burning in the fireplace. They were thinking about launching a search party when the clock went past nine, ten, and then eleven and my grandmother hadn't shown up. The first snow of the season came fast and furious, the dark night becoming even darker with the onset of the snowfall. The neighbors were getting the horses ready and many torches when, just before midnight, my grandmother walked in the yard, very tired, but triumphant and very happy with a small lamb in her arms and the ewe following them. She never viewed the mountain or the mountain animals as hostile. They were extensions of her, the hills and animals a part of her, not foreign, not to be afraid of.

Chapter 10

The small brook next to the meadow was called Koca Dere whose waterfalls were situated a few kilometers from my village. Across a small hanging bridge, which moved like the deck of a boat at sea, up and down with motion of the waves, there were narrow paths leading down to the two small waterfalls and three small pools. The first waterfall was not high, but the pool where the water ended was round and wide and also deep in the middle. There was a nice green meadow, like a green carpet, next to the pool that was a quiet place to sit and let animals graze. The dewdrops on the grass were like jewels in the bright morning rays of sun. The incline from the meadow to the water was a gentle slope, the access to pools easy, and the water was always clean and clear, gradually turning green in the middle. It was a pretty long trek on foot, but I had a good plan in mind. I had the trusted and reliable transportation of Hasan aga's Lightning and I was about the see the most beautiful girl I had ever known. I was so happy and light-hearted, I wanted to sing. I was so excited it felt as if my feet were not touching the ground, as if I were flying like a bird to be with her. That day the singing of the birds had meaning. They sang the song of love for Leyla and me. My Leyla, tall with a narrow waist, white skin that was soft like silk. She was beautiful.

We met in the bus stop and walked slowly along a narrow trail down to the small meadow by the brook. The crashing waterfall made the air smell fresh and cool on a warm, tranquil summer day.

We picked a secluded spot, surrounded by some large cranberry bushes. There on the soft ground covered in grass I spread out my light jacket and invited Leyla to sit. Leyla smiled at me as she sat down. I was nervous to be there alone with her. I sat down next to her and continued to be lost in her eyes. They sparkled with the passion of life. There was nothing in the world, no material possession which I would be willing to exchange for this moment of happiness and the simple joy of being here with Leyla. A fiery, all-consuming passion was awakening like brush fire and I was possessed by it. Keeping eye contact with her, I slowly leaned over to Leyla and kissed her on the cheek and gently moved to her lips. I loved touching and caressing her soft skin. I looked at her eyes and softly said, "I love you. I love you more than anything in the world." I broke my gaze. "I love you so much that I am afraid to hurt you." I slowly withdrew my hand until I stopped touching her completely. But she looked into my eyes and said, "I love you, too, and I trust you. I know that you would not hurt me and you will do nothing stupid." She smiled as she confessed her feelings. I felt a short wave of embarrassment going through me because I had revealed my true feelings for her, but I overcame it quickly and smiled back. It did not matter. The only thing that mattered was our love for each other. I would love her no matter what.

My feelings were stronger than anything I ever had experienced before. They were all encompassing. She moved slowly toward me and gently kissed me on the lips. I responded by pulling her closer to me. I wanted the kiss to never end.

The sky and earth were engaged in their own love conspiracy. They were mischievous witnesses of the love affair of two youths, connecting through an invisible, passionate love. The sky was clear, the day's warmth was washed away by the pleasantly cool breeze off the Rhodope Mountain. Throughout the summer of 1984, we kept meeting and spending time together as the days slipped by.

Chapter 11

I have wings. I fly away like a bird which has been caged for too long. I see the beautiful blue sky, I'm flying high in the warm southern sky. I am one with it, I effortlessly merge with the warm blue. With unbelievable ease, light like a feather, I soar over the tallest buildings and red roofs of Krumovgrad. The picture of the town's roofs and streets from above is so clear and vivid that I am convinced this is real life and I can actually fly like a bird. I am free and carefree, I am happy and timeless. There are no boundaries. Above all, I am with Leyla and she is smiling. She extends her hand and touches my hand, her skin so soft, like fine silk. It feels so real. We hold eye contact. It is so good to be alive and exist. I expand effortlessly, naturally. Again I become one with the universe. It is natural for people to be able to fly in this world. I realize that I am like Icarus, then the feathers of my wings start falling one by one and I am suddenly alarmed and scared. On the way down, thoughts rush through my head. Somehow, somewhere I believe that this is true, somewhere deep inside me is this untold truth, that we all are somehow connected. It is something I feel and my whole body knows it. There is intelligence in my body, beyond my brain and there is intelligence beyond my body in the air, earth and universe, but I don't verbalize my experience. I don't want to be singled out as the strange one, the odd one, the crazy one. Outwardly I try to fit in, to be one of many.

Then with a loud bang I hit the ground and woke up. The bell of my alarm clock had to be one of the most annoying sounds in the universe. I realized that it was a dream. I was a little disappointed, but I told myself that it still was a beautiful dream. I wished it were true. I closed my eyes, wanting to go back to the dream world. Awaking slowly, for a moment I wondered whether I had a dream within a dream, I wondered whether this thing called life was just an illusion. It was my first week back at school and I should strive to be on time.

Bulgarian Communist Party leaders decided that the Turkish language would not be taught in schools any more when I was in junior high school. The purported reason was that the material was too much of a burden for students, but the real reason was to eliminate the Turkish language. Since the a apparatchiks, functionaries, were so *concerned* about the mental well-being of Turkish students, they decided to get rid of all Turkish studies. Off course, this was a pretext, the real reason was the assimilation of the Turks into the Bulgarian majority.

My high school was a big gray building not far from town's center in Krumovgrad. It had been called "gymnasia" by everyone since its inception and there were many classrooms in the building. There were big framed portraits of the general secretaries of the Bulgarian Communist Party and the Soviet Union, Todor Zhivkov and Leonid Brezhnev respectively, at the first floor entrance so we didn't forget who was in charge and running the show in the country.

When I went to Krumovgrad I didn't know most of the students in the high school, but gradually I got to know the other kids, mainly when we played soccer. I was quite good at soccer because we used to play in my village and in my junior high school. We played on big mixed teams of Bulgarian and Turkish students.

The first day of school started with the usual pleasantries; we had to tell about our summer, what we did and what books we read, but our teachers maybe could not understand, or did not want to understand, that when your family farms tobacco in the cooperative there is not much time to read books. I had been busy helping my parents in tobacco plantations and at home processing the tobacco.

That fall we were told by Comrade Dana Kirilova, our class teacher who also taught history and basics of Communism, that there would be heavy emphasis on teaching atheism and anti-capitalism, which in our school also meant anti-Turkish propaganda. The most virulent language was reserved for America.

Our classes were ethnically mixed. In most of the classes, the Turkish students were the majority and Bulgarians, the minority. However, the Bulgarian students always managed to get better grades. A few Turkish students got good grades, too, but they had to work twice as hard.

Comrade Kirilova was in her forties and she was the wife of a Communist functionary. She was deeply indoctrinated in the teachings and principles of Communism, a true believer. Often she wore a red dress, which I guessed symbolized the red flag of Communism, and when she didn't wear her red dress she always wore on her chest a pin of the Soviet flag, the hammer and sickle. She didn't tolerate views that were different from the official party line. Any different opinion was an abomination. She expected the basics of Communism to be studied exactly as they were taught in the textbook and she was vigilant about foreign influences polluting the minds of innocent students.

At school, even if you merely suggested that you believed in Jesus Christ or Allah, you instantly became a target of lengthy harassment by Kirilova and the other teachers.

During one of her classes, Comrade Kirilova, with great self-satisfaction, told us how she and another party functionary from the local town committee of the Communist party went to the local Eastern Orthodox Church and went through the notes the young people left, asking God to help them with the health of their parents or their grades in school. The party functionaries took the notes and left replies that God cannot and will not help them simply because God didn't exist. Then the functionaries hid in the church, waited for the young people to return and they ambushed them, telling them that God would not help them because He didn't exist. At the end of this story, Comrade Kirilova would end up in fits of laughter. She thought she had done a great deed and at the same time she enjoyed crushing the hope of people in need of help.

During our second class for the year, Comrade Kirilova was walking between the rows as usual.

"We will emphasize this semester proof that God or Allah doesn't exist. It was our Communist Party decision that we put emphasis on atheism this season. I will go from student to student and ask what they think about the existence of Allah or God. You need to know that Allah and Jesus Christ are personal enemies of Communism. Religion was created by the people of antiquity as a reaction to suffering and injustice in the world. The oppressed masses were the creators of religion and they used it to reassure themselves that they would have a better existence in the future, in heaven. Religion is like opium for the masses, a way to escape the terrible realities of the world. Also, religion is used in feudal and capitalist societies as a tool of oppression by the ruling class to exploit the masses and keep them under submission."

After this tirade, Comrade Kirilova looked at the class like a victorious Communist leader who had just won a great battle, the battle for the beliefs of the students. Then she looked at us carefully and said, "I will go from student to student and ask, Does Allah exist?" This caused a great deal of consternation among us all and we started to whisper amongst ourselves. I heard a female Turkish student whisper that she believed in the existence of Allah, that there was no way she could say that Allah didn't exist. I was quite worried myself — I didn't want to express my views on the issue. I personally believed in the existence of Allah, but I didn't want to antagonize Comrade Kirilova. My grades depended on her and I had to tell what she wanted to hear.

Comrade Kirilova was not happy with the noise and the reaction of the students. She quickly went to her desk, situated on an elevated podium, and grabbed a stick sitting on the desk, then hit the desk twice. The action sounded like gunshots, which caused the students to quiet. Comrade Kirilova eyed one of the tall girls and said with an iron voice, "Neriman, stand up and tell me, Does Allah exist?" Neriman looked puzzled, as if she was not sure what to say. She stood up and quietly said, "I believe that Allah exists." Comrade Kirilova was infuriated to a boiling point, her face turned red with anger.

"If Allah exists, why doesn't Allah stop me when I give you a failing grade in my notebook?" Comrade Kirilova said angrily, and quickly went to her desk and wrote something in her notebook.

"Neriman, you can sit now. You failed the exam, you failed this class." Then Comrade Kirilova turned to Mehmet who was sitting in the next row. "Mehmet, does Allah exist?" Mehmet looked as puzzled as Neriman. He stood up and looked toward the class, as if he was expecting help from his classmates.

"I don't know," he said quietly, which I thought was quite a slick way to get out of this trap. Unfortunately, this didn't help Mehmet. With lightning speed, Comrade Kirilova delivered a slap to Mehmet's face, and another one to his neck.

"There is no middle way in this business," she said. Then she asked the next student, who said that Allah didn't exist. Since no one wanted to be beaten in front of the whole class or get a failing grade, no one dared oppose Comrade Kirilova. The rest of the students simply started saying, "No, Allah doesn't exist."

I was grateful that I was sitting in the back and didn't get slapped in the face. I, too, said no, even though I thought otherwise. I realized that things had changed for the worse. Our teachers had previously been adamant in teaching their Marxism and Leninism, and everything that came with it, but this year they were militant about it. We were in serious trouble.

*   *   *

I met Bekir my first year of school in Krumovgrad and I considered him a good friend. He was born in town, his parents moving there from one of the villages not far away. He was intelligent and I liked to talk to him about current events. Like me, he enjoyed reading books. He was tall and skinny with a lively look on his face. It had been my observation that the town kids were often aloof and lacking good manners. At the beginning of my time at the school, they were distant. We, the village kids, taught them how to greet and shake hands and make small talk so we could get to know each other. Our good manners wore off on them, even though they were supposed to be more sophisticated than we were. The town kids knew more, they had access to the town and school libraries throughout the entire year, they could read newspapers and magazines every day, but their social skills were poor.

During one of the recesses, I talked to Bekir.

"Hello, Bekir, how are you?" I said with firmness in my voice and reached to shake his hand.

"I am doing well," he said, as he took my hand.

"How was your summer?" I asked him.

"Pretty good," he replied.

"Did you have time to read some books?"

"Oh, yeah, I read many good books this summer. How about you?"

I responded, smiling, "I read a few. I have been busy working in the tobacco fields. I helped my parents with the tobacco, which took most of my summer."

Then Bekir leaned in and whispered, "My parents heard that there will be immigration to Turkey sometime soon. They want to move to Turkey so they can avoid the name change." I saw that he was serious and believed in what he said. I didn't want to be too direct and hurt his feelings, but the truth had to be told.

"If there will be immigration, why are they changing the names from Turkish to Bulgarian? Are they going to send people to Turkey with new Bulgarian names? What you are saying doesn't make sense?"

"My parents heard that the name change will stop south and east of the town, that the Turks of Krumovgrad will be allowed to move to Turkey."

"Why they would stop just outside the town?"

Bekir responded with conviction in his voice. "That was what my parents believe, I believe it, too."

"I hope you are right, because that means we will be eligible to immigrate to Turkey as well. My parents want to move to Turkey, too." What Bekir said sounded like wishful thinking to me, but I didn't want to dash his hopes. Then I heard the bell ring, recess was over, and we went to our seats in class.

Comrade Kirilova entered the classroom with her usual pride, which I interpreted as arrogance. She looked at the class as if she could read our thoughts. All her behavior probably was just a façade, but it was unpleasant and irritating. She didn't impress many. She taught Basics of Communism, which was not one of my favorite classes. With the advance of the name change campaign, everything Comrade Kirilova taught in this class sounded fake and hollow. They were teaching one thing and doing another.

Comrade Kirilova started walking slowly between the rows of sitting students, all dressed in blue. When she approached Bekir's table, she noticed that he was scribbling something on his notebook. She approached Bekir from the back and looked at the writing and then all hell broke loose. Comrade Kirilova screamed like a hog being slaughtered for Eastern Orthodox Christmas. With a swift motion, she grabbed Bekir's notebook.

"What is this on the drawing? Is this the moon and crescent of the Turkish flag?" she asked in her stern voice.

"No, I am drawing the hammer and sickle of the Soviet flag," Bekir said innocently.

"What does the sign under the drawing say? Is this in Turkish?" she demanded. Bekir said nothing, just stood there calmly.

"Does it say Turkey? The sign is in Turkish?" Comrade Kirilova asked again, in an icy tone.

She grabbed Bekir by the arm and said in a voice that would not tolerate opposition, "We are going to the principal's office." She practically dragged him out of class, and we were all puzzled as to what the fuss was all about.

After an hour, Bekir made it back from the principal's office where he had been questioned about the picture. Comrade Kirilova thought that Bekir was drawing the Turkish flag with the moon and crescent, but Bekir insisted all the time that he was drawing the hammer and sickle and he was going to write "Soviet Union" after "long live." Bekir was taken back to the principal's office. That was the last time I saw him. Later I heard that the sign said in Turkish, "Long live Turkey." He was taken to the local police office where he was beaten mercilessly by half a dozen police officers with masks. His almost-dead body was thrown on the street.

Passers-by recognized him and they carried him home where he barely survived the cruel beating. Then I knew that we Turks of Bulgaria were in dire straits. Communism was going to show its true face. A few days later, when the wave of the name change campaign hit Krumovgrad, Bekir was arrested and sent to the concentration camp in Belene.

I was torn between what I was told in school and what I was taught at home. At school, they taught that religion was the tool of capitalism that kept the masses pacified like sheep, as the "great" theorist of Communism Karl Marx said, "Religion is the opiate of the people."

There were many kids who could not make themselves say that they did not believe in Allah, and they ended up on a special list. They were treated worse than the rest of the students, and would get lower grades and even beatings would be administered, as beating students was permitted and encouraged as a disciplinary tool in Bulgaria.

In late 1970s the Bulgarian authorities stopped teaching Turkish language in the schools. In early 1980, the number of Turkish books dwindled in Bulgarian bookstores, and by 1984 they had completely disappeared from the bookstores and libraries. All Turkish literature was burned in big piles, which was curiously reminiscent of the book burning by the Nazis in Nazi Germany. After the name change campaign, authorities went from house to house of the Turks and collected all the Turkish language books and burned them. As Heinrich Heine said, "Where one burns books, one will soon burn people." This phrase became a reality in Bulgaria.

We had a male teacher, Todor Bokov, who I thought grim and unfriendly. He spent most of his time in the basement where he taught trudovo, shop class. I heard rumors that he and another male teacher would gather Turkish students they disliked for one reason or another and beat them with sticks in the basement.

Not all teachers, however, were like Comrade Kirilova and Bokov. Ognian Petrov was a young, blue-eyed, handsome man and an intelligent and independent thinker. He would engage with us in conversations about personal matters, like personal grooming, high fashion and travel. He liked to dress well. He didn't mind being seen wearing jeans, even though jeans were considered a Western influence and were frowned upon by the Communist apparatchiks. We liked him because he was friendly and open-minded, he treated us with respect, as equals, as though we were worthy to be talked to and listened to. We appreciated this greatly. Our fragile self-esteem moved up a notch around him. We even suspected that he was one of the closet pro-Western teachers; he didn't verbalize his opinions on everything openly, but from his grooming and his reluctance to agree enthusiastically with the views of the Communist leaders, we felt that he liked the West and most of what the West had to offer, like material wealth and ideology. We could openly talk with Ognian about a wide variety of topics which didn't exclude international politics. His views diverged from the mainstream Communist line.

Many of the teachers, like Comrades Kirilova and Bokov, were mini Stalins — it was their way or the highway. "You are not mature enough to think with your own heads" was by them repeated as a mantra. We were told we didn't even need to think with our own heads because the great Bulgarian Communist Party, and of course, its great leader, Todor Zhivkov, had all the answers and did all the thinking for us. "So rest assured you are in good hands," they would tell us, "just follow the party instructions." The high school was the place to learn Communist ideology, be obedient and strictly follow the party orders, stay passive, don't cause trouble for the Communist party and system, don't raise any questions. All those immature souls graduating from high school at age 18 suddenly, as if by magic, became mature because the party decided so and wrote as much in the diplomas of the graduating students.

Chapter 12

It was a quiet autumn Saturday day in Çaliköy. I was back from school for the weekend, because we didn't have classes on Saturday and Sunday. I had heard rumors that the name change campaign was advancing slowly but surely toward our village. Everybody was talking only about the campaign.

The wind had increased since late afternoon and was pushing the clouds faster and faster, but I could not predict the coming storm. My mother was cooking çorba, soup, on the woodburning stove in the kitchen, which was also my parents' bedroom. I was switching between listening to the Voice of America and Radio Free Europe on their portable, Russian-made VEF transistor radio. The event of the forceful name change campaign was attracting the attention of Western governments and news media.

There were rumors that the names of the Turks would be changed in certain remote border villages, and the name change campaign would stop east and south of us. This line of deception continually moved toward our village. At a certain moment, we realized that the line would move through our village, and we knew then the rumors about the end of the campaign had been spread by the ruling Communist party so they could keep passive the people whose names had not yet been changed.

When the name change campaign accelerated in the second half of 1984, my friend Mustafa and I would often take my father's transistor radio to listen to the broadcasts of BBC London, Voice of America, and Radio Free Europe in the meadow behind the village, in our yard or, on nights like this, when it was windy and cloudy with a storm gathering, in my room. We were happy that the free world was getting the news of the terrible oppression in Bulgaria. It was a great morale boost for us; we knew that we were not alone in the struggle for our rights.

What the Bulgarian Communist Party leaders were saying about the name change campaign did not match reality in the country. Bulgarian Communist leaders repeated the lie that the Turks were changing their names on a voluntary basis. It was uplifting that the most powerful democracies were standing up for us as the lies of the Communist party were revealed by the Western media. In the following years, the international community would increase the pressure on the Bulgarian government to force them to change their stance on the Turkish minority in the country.

I listened to the VOA's program in special English, with the radio broadcaster speaking slowly so people who were new to the English language could understand the news. I was so keen to understand what the VOA was saying that I found an English textbook after a long search and started to teach myself.

I could listen to the radio when my father was not listening to the news from Turkey. He had increasing difficulty listening to their radio broadcasts, however, because more and more often the broadcasts were jammed by huge antennas built in the early 1980s on top of some of the highest hills of the eastern Rhodope Mountains. The purpose of the jamming stations was to suppress the broadcasts of Radio Free Europe in the Bulgarian language, BBC London in Bulgarian and Turkish, all Turkish-speaking radio stations, and TV broadcasts from Turkey — all those who were telling the truth about the events of the forced name change of Turks. The broadcasts were jammed with a buzzing sound transmitted on the same radio wave lengths.

My parents were getting ready for supper when I heard a loud banging on the outside door.

My father jumped up and headed toward the house's entrance door. I turned off the radio in my room and rushed out to the foyer, too.

At the door we saw a man named Veli, whom we knew from the village. He was breathing heavily and was clearly distraught.

"Kazim aga, there is a long column of military trucks, jeeps, and tanks moving toward Ada. I was returning late from collecting wood on the hills surrounding the village when I saw the column. They are going to force the Turks in Ada to accept Bulgarian names tonight."

"Oh, God," said my father with fear in his voice. "If they are changing the names in Ada then our turn is next."

"Kazim aga, maybe we should run for the hills," Veli said eagerly.

"But how long we will be running and hiding?" asked my father. "How we can live in the mountains with winter approaching? The villagers south of us ran and hid in the mountains all summer long, but all of them were hunted down and their names changed anyway, and in the process they suffered horrendous beatings. The Bulgarian Communist military and police have the weapons. What have we to resist them — nothing but our bare hands? We should not resist."

Veli's jaw dropped, because what he had heard my father say was something completely unexpected and shocking.

"It is obvious," my father continued, "that they have decided to change the names of all Turks in Bulgaria. The palnomoshtnik, mayor, told me the authorities will be changing the names of Turks everywhere, and that the police and soldiers are authorized to shoot and kill anyone who resists. There is no need for people to get hurt from the inevitable. This problem will be solved through peaceful political process, not through violence."

Veli was speechless. He looked at my father's face with disbelieving eyes, wondering how this man could preach nonviolence when the authorities were coming for us armed with everything they had.

My father was a man who liked to take the middle way when possible. When I now think about him, he was level-headed and shunned sudden action. He liked to think things over before he acted. I understood only later how difficult the cataclysm of the name change campaign and my rushed actions must have been on him. But right then, I realized that the Bulgarian Communist government had lost its legitimacy, and the war for the hearts and minds of the Turks was lost, too. When I heard what Veli said, my heart sank with fear for Leyla. I had this gut feeling that something horrible was going to happen to her. Suddenly, the world felt darker and ominous, and breathing became more difficult, as if somebody had snatched the oxygen from the air. I had to go to warn her, but I could not tell my father because he would not have allowed it. I decided that the best plan would be to sneak out and take Lightning.

While my father was still talking to Veli, I snuck out of the house and ran to the barn where Lightning was kept. I threw open the door and grabbed the saddle, walking as fast as I could toward Lightning. The young stallion was startled and started pawing the floor, looking at me as though he wanted to say, "What is going on? What is this commotion about?" I threw the horse blanket and saddle on his back and cinched up the saddle around his belly. I put my left foot on the stirrup and threw my right leg up over his back. I dug my heels into his side and we were off. My eyes adjusted to the moonlight, and I was able to see far into the night.

Lightning was as fast as ever. On the long, narrow and downhill road, we headed into the night, to Ada. I was able to see my way in the bright moments when the moon would jump out between the clouds, but it also helped that Lightning remembered this narrow path from previous trips.

In no time we approached the village from the south bank of Arda River. I decided it would be quieter to walk without Lightning, so I tied him to a tree near the water fountain where we had met Leyla before. I caressed Lightning gently on the neck and whispered in his ear.

"I will be back soon. Please keep quiet."

I knew this place well; I used to come here to swim and fish in the river. My family also used to come here to work in the tobacco fields, so I was confident that I could find my way back to Lightning in the dark. The clouds in the sky were getting darker, which would provide some cover.

I wanted to get to the village without being noticed by the militia, the police, or the soldiers. I knew that on this side of the village there were many fenced gardens where people of the village grew vegetables. I decided to walk through the gardens to get to the edge of the village and slip inside without being noticed. I knew the exact location of Leyla's house. The window facing the street was her room and I intended to go and knock on the window.

First, I climbed the hill by the village so I could see where the soldiers and police were situated. As I got closer, I could hear the noise of Soviet-made, armored personnel carriers. My blood froze when I heard sporadic shooting. I wondered if the shots had killed any of the Turks living in the village. Most of the military trucks were on the outskirts of the village, and I decided I could go through the gardens. I walked slowly toward the houses, keeping an eye out for any patroling soldiers, and kept my head low as I climbed the crude stone fence. Once over, I could see the water fountain built to water the gardens and livestock. There were different sections in the water reservoirs for animals to drink and for villagers to get water with buckets or attach a hose to the fountain. The water fountain was built in a small area protected by some trees on the side of a small hill. I realized the militia and soldiers hadn't reached this area of the village, and I knew I had little time. I decided to run along the empty narrow road instead of climbing the fences and walking through the gardens. I ran fast, as if my life depended on it, and as I approached Leyla's house I was relieved to see that her window was lit. Without any hesitation, I knocked on the window. I couldn't see inside, as the curtain was closed. I knocked again, this time louder. Then the curtain slowly moved and there was Leyla. When she saw my face, she opened the window. I wanted to hug her, but I just said, "Leyla, I need to tell you something urgently. Could you come outside?"

She didn't hesitate for long and she jumped from the window, as it was low to the ground.

"Leyla, the soldiers are coming here to change your names," I said breathlessly, standing there and leaning slightly toward her. "I wanted to tell you before they come, so you and your parents are not startled. I heard the noise of their trucks outside the village."

"What are we going to do now?" She asked with tension in her voice.

As we were standing there, we suddenly saw a dark figure approaching us from the shadows. One of the soldiers, holding a machine gun in hand, was coming toward us.

"Osman," the soldier said with a firm voice. I froze. He knew my name? The voice sounded familiar and I looked carefully when the moon showed from behind the clouds. I was shocked to recognize the soldier—he was the nasty teacher from my high school, Todor Bokov. He was a zapastniak-reservist, police officer, coming here to change the names of the Turks. My blood boiled with anger. I had Leyla with me and I could not let anything happen to her. I felt that I had led her and myself into a trap. But Bokov didn't know I was determined to take Leyla to safety no matter what happened.

With the courage I got from my love, I threw myself forward toward Bokov. He didn't have time to lift the machine gun. I got hold of the gun, pulled Bokov toward me, and with lightning speed, smashed my forehead into his face. He didn't expect the attack and his hold of the gun loosened. He was dazed from the unexpected blow, and I was able quickly to wrestle the gun from his hand. I turned the butt of the gun toward his forehead and delivered another blow, hard enough to render him unconscious. While Bokov was slowly dropping to the ground, I threw the gun away and

102

grabbed Leyla's hand.

"Run with me," I said. "You witnessed the incident — they could go after you, too."

Leyla didn't hesitate and we ran together toward Lightning, visible in the distance. Not far from Lightning we saw another dark figure wandering in the night. At first I thought it was another zapastniak, and I was afraid. I wanted to avoid another confrontation. I looked more carefully and I realized it was not zapastniak. It was somebody from the village. The man was distressed, he looked lost, he didn't know where he was going or what he was doing.

I carefully walked through the tobacco field and slowly approached the man. When the moonlight was brighter between clouds, I was able to recognize that the man was Ramazan hoca from the mosque in Ada. He was walking aimlessly, his eyes wide open, and he was making strange sounds, crying and mumbling and talking to himself. I was glad to see somebody I knew and could trust. I wanted to ask Ramazan hoca what was going on in the village.

"Hello, Ramazan hoca," I said respectfully and in as low a voice as possible. "What is happening in Ada?"

"Don't ask, my son, don't ask. I saw a glimpse of hell tonight, hell on earth. Oglum, my son, there is no Allah," Ramazan said in a cracking dry voice. "I prayed a thousand times so they wouldn't do this to us, so the Bulgarian Communists wouldn't change our Muslim Turkish names to Bulgarian ones, and that they wouldn't inflict any harm on the Turks living in Bulgaria. I prayed and prayed, but all of it was in vain. If Allah is up there and watching over us, why would Allah allow things like this to

103

happen to us? Why? The soldiers have come to change our names. I ask why Allah allows such a thing to happen? Why?" Ramazan hoca was looking at me with the wide-open eyes of a crazy man, a man who had lost his faith and was slowly losing his mind.

All this was like a black-and-white movie being played in slow motion. It took time for the blasphemous words from a priest to form meaning in my head. They were so distressing. The very soul of this man was wounded, and I didn't know how to respond. How could I understand somebody who suffered a deeper pain and anguish than I had ever known? How can one help somebody who had lost all his faith in humanity and God? How I could encourage him? I simply didn't know. All I wanted was to get out of there. I felt deep pity for Ramazan hoca, and an unbearable pain welled up inside me for the people in Ada. Ramazan hoca had always smiled and helped people whenever he could, he had never lost his temper or cursed, and he was always positive, polite, and happy. I was saddened that a man like Ramazan hoca was so distressed, but I had to take Leyla to Çaliköy to get her to safety as soon as possible.

The cries of Ramazan hoca reverberated late into the night. He was walking now aimlessly and shouting, "There is no Allah, Allah doesn't exist."

We walked on, and when Lightning was in sight, we walked faster. I put Leyla on his back behind the saddle and I mounted myself. I told her to hang on tight, I dug my heels into Lightning's side, and we flew back home. The storm which had been gathering power all night finally let loose with a bright flash and a tremendous crack of thunder, as big rain drops fell down to earth.

With the sudden onset of the storm, I slowed Lightning down so he would not slip on the path between our villages. I went straight to Mustafa's house. We were completely soaked from the torrential rain, but I was greatly relieved that we made it. I whistled our signal outside Mustafa's house and soon he came outside. I told him everything about my encounter with the zapastniak and Leyla witnessing the incident and the meeting with Ramazan, who was losing his mind and walking aimlessly in the fields by the river.

"What are we going to do now?" I asked Mustafa in bewilderment as I helped Leyla down from Lightning's back. I turned to look at him, waiting for an answer to the question.

"This is not good," Mustafa said, dread written on his face. "The zapaztniak have seen your face and they will probably recognize you. They will soon come looking for you."

"We need to go to Hasan aga," Mustafa continued. "He is a smart, tough guy and will know what to do. He might be able to help hide Leyla around here until this affair is over."

We went straight to Hasan's house and knocked on the door and he soon appeared. Nowadays, people didn't sleep very much or too deeply, with the worry about the name change campaign squeezing everyone's hearts. People were jumpy; they expected the militia and zapastniaks to knock on their doors any moment. I filled Hasan in about everything that had happened and asked him if he could help hide Leyla. Behind Hasan, Fidan looked on with curiosity. When she saw Leyla distressed she said, "Poor thing! How are you? Are you well?" Leyla was dazed from the unexpected drama and only an unclear mumbling came out of her.

"Come inside, let me see you," Fidan said and she gently helped Leyla inside.

Hasan looked straight into my eyes and said, "Now, we can hide Leyla here in my house and later, when this turmoil passes, we will send her back to her parents. My advice to you, Osman, is to run far away. I mean out of Bulgaria, otherwise the militia will catch you and they could kill you for resisting the name change campaign."

Hasan looked at us grimly.

"Listen to me carefully," Hasan said. "I have a friend, a Pomak, a Bulgarian Mohammedan. He lives close to the Greek border. His name is Ömer and he knows the border very well. He knows how the installations on the border work and what places are mined. The Bulgarian–Greek border is called the Iron Curtain for a reason, because it is difficult to cross illegally. There are extensive areas that are mined. If you get in one of those fields, you probably will not survive.

"But Ömer knows exactly where to safely cross the border," Hasan continued. "He goes inside the border almost daily in the summer because they have tobacco fields inside the border fence. The border guards do not let the farm tractor drivers in, since they do not know them. Therefore, the few people who own fields inside the border have to plow with oxen. They can sneak you through when they cross with oxcarts. I will tell you exactly how to get to Ömer's village and how to find his house. We have been working together for many years cutting wood in the mountains by his village. We are like brothers. He trusts me, and I trust him with my life, and I have no doubt he will be able to help you."

I trusted Hasan because he and my father were like brothers and he treated me as if I were his son. I had heard stories from my friends discussing the Bulgarian-Greek border that there were two parallel sets of fences throughout the whole length of the border. The distance from the first barbed wire fence to the second one could be up to three kilometers, in other places even more. The reason for this distance was that a border violator was expected to trip the electronic alarm going through the first barbed wire fence, thereby giving enough time for the border patrol to get between the escapee and the second barbed wire fence. Once they spotted the violator, the border guards could catch him or shoot him.

"Brother, I am going with you," Mustafa suddenly said. "There is no life for us here. I cannot stay here." I looked at him, stunned. "It will be less scary for you, and two sets of eyes can see better than one," he continued.

For a while I didn't know what to say. Upon recovering from the shock of Mustafa's words I said, "No, you should not come with me, because it will be extremely dangerous. It is possible we could get shot."

"You can't stop me," Mustafa said in a firm voice. "Better dead than in endless slavery to the Commies."

Inside I wanted Mustafa to go with me because I did not want to leave him behind and lose my friend. He had been my best friend since our childhood. We had grown up together playing çelik, and hide and seek. I trusted him with my life. But at the same time I felt responsible for his well-being. How I could look Mustafa's parents in the eyes if something happened to him while escaping through the border?

When Mustafa decided something, however, there was no stopping him. At times he could be stubborn like a donkey. As the old Turkish saying goes, the blood which was meant to be spilled will not stay in the vein. The decision was made, and we were going together.

"There is a small problem, though," I said. "My father will never agree to let me to cross the border illegally."

"Don't worry about that," Hasan said resolutely. "I will take care of it now. I will go and talk to your father." Hasan was tough, as tough they came around here. We all went to our house together, and Hasan knocked on the door loudly. My father showed up after a brief moment. He was sleepy and dazed, and was probably wondering what all this commotion was about. Hasan quickly told my father the bad news. He looked to Hasan then to me, then back to Hassan. He had the face of a person who was in utter shock. In the end, Hasan insisted that I escape from the country immediately.

"Osman only has one chance to stay alive or stay out of jail — he has to make it to the other side of the border," Hasan said. My father looked at Hasan with a stern expression, his eyes flashing with anger.

"I have only one son," he said, "and I want him to stay with us. Whatever happens, let it happen. If he stays with us he will not be killed at the border. Osman isn't going anywhere!"

Hasan would not take no for an answer. "I want to talk to you in private," he said quietly and they went into another room. Mustafa and I waited, standing in the foyer of the house. At first the talk inside was muffled, but with time it become louder as Hasan worked to convince my father. It was obvious that my father was resisting, but Hasan was resolute and the more my father resisted the louder Hasan got. After a while there was silence inside and then my father appeared at the door. He didn't make eye contact at first, but after a while he slowly lifted his gaze and said, "Go, Osman, go, my son."

I have often wondered what Hasan said to my father that made him change his mind so quickly, knowing that my father was not a man to be easily swayed.

While we prepared to escape, gathering supplies needed to get through the fence, Leyla was on my mind. I wanted to see her, talk to her one last time. I told my parents that I would be right back. I quickly walked to Hasan's house and knocked on the door. Fidan opened the door, her eyes wide with fear and anxiety written on her face.

"Fidan abla, I need to see Leyla," I said hastily, using the term of respect afforded older women. "I need to say goodbye to Leyla."

Fidan opened the door so I could pass and pointed toward the kitchen door. I entered the small kitchen and saw Leyla was covered with a blanket, sitting next to the woodburning stove, cold and in shock.

"Leyla, are you all right?" I asked quietly, kneeling beside her.

"I don't feel well," Leyla said, meeting my gaze. "I am cold and I can't get warm." The events of the evening had caught up with her, affecting her more than the cold or damp. I could see the fear and worry in her eyes, caused by the presence of the military and police in her village.

"I am sorry you are so cold," I told her. "Hasan aga thinks I must escape to Greece; otherwise, he thinks if I am arrested by the military or the police I will be killed, or in the best case imprisoned for a long time. I think I should take his advice and escape. I wish you could come with me, but I think you will be safer here, without me," I said, truly wishing that she could go with me.

"I will miss you, but I think you should go, too, and I don't think I can go with you because I am exhausted and I would only be a burden to you," Leyla said quietly.

I was worried about her well-being, but if she developed a bad cold in the mountains or was unable to walk, then we both would be easily hunted down by the police or border guards. At this point I wanted to escape, because we had no rights left in this country. If being Turkish was unacceptable to the rulers of this country, then this country was the wrong place to live. My heart was breaking, however, that I had to leave Leyla. I loved her so much, and my parents, relatives, friends, and neighbors. I was leaving behind everyone I had ever known.

I looked at Leyla with tears in my eyes and quietly said, "Goodbye, my love, I will never forget you."

"Goodbye, Osman, I, too, will always remember you," Leyla said, with tears running down her face. We hugged and kissed for not nearly long enough. It was time for me to leave the village for the Greek border.

Chapter 13

Mustafa and I quickly left our village. My father and mother had only enough time to say goodbye to me. They embraced and kissed Mustafa and me on the cheeks, and wished us well in the traditional Turkish way, "May your path be open, and good luck." The raid of the village Ada and our escape was happening so fast that my parents felt bewildered and scared for my life and well-being. According to another old Turkish saying, You can leave and never return; return and never find the people you left behind. My parents did not know what the future would hold for me or for them. They were happy I had been able to escape from the zapastniak reservist and that Leyla and I had run away unharmed, but now they were scared that the authorities might find me. I turned back and looked at them for a last time. They looked as if they had lost everything worth living for in the world, and I could see deepest anguish on both of their faces. I felt pity and shame that I was putting them through this experience.

It was hard for me to wrap my head around the events of the night. It was surreal. I didn't know whether I could do it on my own. I had never lived outside of our village without my parents. Could I live by myself? I didn't know where I was going or what I was going to do there. All I knew was that I had to go if I wanted to remain alive and out of a Communist camp or prison.

My heart was breaking, but I did not have a choice if I wanted to live. It was either surrender and risk being killed or spend years, maybe the rest of my life, in prison or a death camp — or flee the country and live free, but alone.

On this, my last night in my village, my home, I knew I would never experience our old house or the village like this again, with the sounds of nature and the animals, and people happily anticipating another busy summer day.

Mustafa and I left our village with a small bag of food, clothes, folding knife and pliers. As the thunderstorm ended, we rode Lightning fast on remote shepherd trails, south toward the border. We could not use the roads, or even travel close to the roads for fear of being seen by police. Hope and fear gripped my heart, and I realized I had put all our families' lives in danger, Mustafa's, Ömer's, and mine. There was no easy way to hide a horse and its riders, and police looking for us would have no problem spotting us from a distance.

Suddenly in the distance I heard the faint noise of an engine, louder than a police truck and high in the sky — a military helicopter approaching fast. My heart hammered as I looked for a place to hide, but there was not a single tree or bush or cave anywhere. I spurred Lightning to a full gallop and we flew across the field. I buried my face in Lightning's thick mane to cut wind resistance, and Mustafa leaned on my back, but we were no match for the speed of the helicopter which descended upon us like an angry eagle. The soldiers opened fire and bullets whooshed by us as I steered Lightning zigzag to a dry riverbed of small stones. Lightning lost his balance and we all collapsed in a big could of dust and stones.

The helicopter ominously turned in a circle over us, sure they had hit us, stirring up a big cloud of dust that hid us. I undid Lightning's headstall and saddle fast and turned him loose. I knew he would find his way home. As the helicopter approached the ground, its tail rotor hit a tree and broke into pieces. The helicopter spun violently and crashed into the ground, causing the earth to shake from the impact. The main rotor broke into pieces that were flung all over the surrounding area. Mustafa and I were knocked down from the shock wave as the helicopter exploded and everything caught fire. There was no way any of our attackers could have survived the horrible accident.

We were scared witless and decided to leave the scene as fast as we could and took off toward Ömer's village. Lightning headed a different way, toward home.

When the reinforcements arrived, they would find only the remains of the burned helicopter and charred bodies of the people in the aircraft. There would be no trace of Mustafa, me, or Lightning. All of us would be gone. I grabbed our small bag with food and tools, while Mustafa hid the saddle in the bushes nearby.

We headed east toward Ömer's village. We had to get there fast because there would soon be many police officers and military looking for us. We ran as fast as we could. After about an hour of nonstop running we had to slow down. We also had to make sure we were moving in the right direction. The sun was climbing in the eastern sky in the direction of

Ömer's village. South was the border and I knew we were pretty close now. We didn't know whether the police and military had known we were headed south to the Greek border, or if the helicopter had discovered us by chance. The good part for us was that by turning east, parallel to the border, we would avoid the search parties headed south to search for us. They would not expect us to turn east and walk about ten kilometers to Ömer's village before turning south again toward the border. We walked in silence, fearful and anxious.

According to my calculations, I thought we should be getting close to Ömer's village. We bypassed the small hamlets strewn on the rolling hills of the eastern Rhodope Mountains. The village we were headed to should be past a high hill in front of us. This part of the mountains was forested, which offered some protection, but after the helicopter crash everything looked hostile and we thought that behind every bush there was a soldier or hidden trap. We needed to be careful not to be seen going into Ömer's house. We could not afford to get Ömer and his family in trouble.

They had suffered enough in the 1970s. Ömer and his family and all other Pomaks living in Bulgaria went through the same fate as the Turks in the 1980s. Their Turkish-Islamic names were changed forcefully to Bulgarian by the Bulgarian Communist Party. Many Pomaks were killed in the process or imprisoned. They numbered more than 250,000 in Bulgaria, a smaller minority than Turks. Most of them lived in small villages by the southern border of Bulgaria.

We headed for the hilltop. When we got there, we saw the village below in a small valley. The houses were small and all of their roofs were covered with big flat stones, not red tiles like the houses in our village. For the first time we could see the border fence, built of barbed wire. The fence glided like a serpent over the gently sloping green hills of the mountains. We decided to wait on top of the hill for night; we were more tired than hungry. From that location we could see the narrow asphalt road that led to the village. The road was between us and the border fence. If we followed Hasan's instructions carefully, we would not have a problem finding Ömer's house, but we had to wait for it to get dark so no one could see us. We were putting not only our lives in danger, but Ömer's life as well.

The weather was nice, sunny and warm, and we were exhausted from our eventful night trip. We decided it was a safe place to sleep. We were too far from the village, the border and road to be detected, and the grass there was tall and soft. It didn't take us long to fall asleep. When we woke up, it was getting dark. I felt dazed and disoriented for few moments after awakening. I thought what had happened to us was not real, it was just a nightmare, but the more awake I became the more I realized that everything had really happened. I had regret and fear for Leyla and our families, and anxiety about crossing the border. I tried to chase the annoying thoughts away, but they came back with more power. Mustafa woke up not long after me. He was sullen and serious, his body slumped. We ate the remaining food as we waited for full dark.

By eight o'clock, it was completely dark. We had been looking at the road leading to the village, a narrow strip of asphalt, and we were about to head for the village when we heard the thunder of big military trucks approaching. We looked at each other and lay low behind tall grass.

"It doesn't look good," I whispered to Mustafa. "It looks as if they are sending extra guards to the border."

"Maybe we should not go to the village," he replied.

"Yes, maybe we shouldn't." My body was tense from fear and anxiety, about being on our own and not risking the lives of Ömer and his family. We needed to cross the border soon before even more soldiers arrived and it became impossible to cross.

The no man's land between the two fences of the border was surrounded by forest, but there were no trees between the two fences. Those trees had all been cut down so the guards could see and stop defectors inside the border area. I had heard stories about many young Turkish and Pomak boys who had escaped in the 1960s and now lived in America, Australia, or Turkey. I had heard it was easier to escape then. The border fence with barbed wire was built and fortified to its current form in the 1970s, under the guidance of the Soviet military.

The son of a Bulgarian military officer from my high school had told me that in the 1970s and 1980s, many East German and other Eastern Europeans, mainly teenagers, had been caught at the border. Some had been executed on the spot and their bodies were buried in unmarked graves. The border guards, who were conscripted like the rest of the Bulgarian military, were rewarded with vacations for killing border violators. The guards had also started laying land mines west of us, where it seemed that some people had managed to escape from the name change campaign. Eventually they would mine this part of the border, too. My high school friend knew all this from one of the commanders of the border guards, stationed not far from the villages.

We were in the right position to cross the border. We decided to wait until past midnight, thinking that the border guards would be tired and the patrols less frequent.

"I wonder how many youth have been killed on this border throughout the years, trying to escape to freedom. I am thinking hundreds, maybe thousands, across the entire length of the Iron Curtain." I vocalized my morbid thought.

"That's a crazy thing to think about before crossing the Iron Curtain," Mustafa said, despondent. He had a difficult time hiding the jitters eating at him from inside. I knew it was a morbid thing to think about, but it was a very real possibility that we could be shot dead and no one would find out about it if the guards decided so. Communist rulers didn't want to advertise that people were trying to escape from Communist *paradise*.

The term Iron Curtain was embedded in my memory by Radio Free Europe's continued repetitions of the term in Bulgarian language. They repeated the term almost every night. Now I was next to the Iron Curtain, watching it, attempting to breach it. It was one of the coldest and loneliest places on the earth anyone could imagine. There were no people, not even animals, on that long stretch of land, except a group of reluctant guards. The Iron Curtain was built not to stop potential intruders, but to stop people living within the boundaries of the country from fleeing. Many more people than ever before were interested in escaping. We were two of those souls.

From the woods where we were hidden, I could see the first barbed wire fence of the Iron Curtain. I had been staring at the point where we would start digging, as if by a magical force I could make the barbed wire disappear, or at least open, so I could walk through easily. I was also thinking that it would be difficult to cross the border, but not impossible.

I couldn't stop myself from dwelling on the brave people who had been killed at this border, killed while trying to escape to freedom. It was an odd thing to think about when I was about to attempt to cross illegally myself. I could not help but think about these things. After all the stories I had heard about people being shot or blown to pieces by the mines, I was scared. My breathing was short and heavy, and it felt as if there was not enough oxygen in the air.

It was getting cooler now. The fall days were warm and pleasant, but the nights were cool, especially there in the higher peaks of the mountain.

While I was lying there eyeing the border, I remembered the story about how a Pomak's donkey somehow ended up inside the no man's land between the two barbed wires fences; most likely the owner had forgotten about the animal. During the night, the donkey looked for a way to go home and bumped the border wire repeatedly. The alarm was set off and the border guards rushed out, but they could not see the animal in the dark. They thought there was a violator trying to cross the border. They ordered the violator to stop, but he would not stop moving. The border guards opened fire and the shooting continued for three hours until morning came. There, in the morning light, was the donkey, still alive and well, inside the border. After that event the commander of the unit was demoted. Maybe in the end those border guards were not that good. Spreading lies and misinformation, in this case spreading scary stories, was one of the ways to keep people from escaping to freedom.

I looked at my Soviet-made watch; it was past midnight. It was time to go. I reached for the pocketknife, signaled to Mustafa, and we moved slowly toward the fence. My eyes were adjusted to the dark. The night was not too cloudy, and I could see the moon and the stars staring at us with curiosity, wanting to say, "What do you think that you are doing?" It took us about ten minutes to dig under the wire, but it felt like an eternity. This was a lower location, between two small hills. If there were border guards somewhere there, they would not see me, but I could not see them, either. I finished digging the hole and I pushed my body inside, crawling on my hands and knees, into no man's land. Then Mustafa made it through the hole without much effort. My heart was beating like a drum in my chest, prompting and urging me to go, go, go. I walked hunched over, followed closely by Mustafa, slowly in the beginning and then faster and faster, toward the high mountain peak we saw on the horizon.

Suddenly I could see the border's plowed furrow in front of me, about ten meters wide. I was prepared for it. The border furrow was a continuous stretch of land that had been tilled inside the border so the guards could see if there had been violators inside and the direction they went. I had brought a couple of small branches from the hill. I turned my back to the south and start walking backward, Mustafa now walking in front of me. I bent, and with the branches, erased our footprints from the tilled soil. When I reached the other side, I walked for a while and then hid the tree branches in the tall grass, before I continued walking south.

Once, when I was in school, we visited the ruins of an old castle situated on one of the highest peaks of the eastern Rhodope Mountains. One of the boys who wanted to show us how knowledgeable he was in local geography pointed toward the mountain peak situated south of us.

"See that peak over there? That is in Greece. The border is at the bottom of that hill." I remembered where that hill was. I could see the peak in front of me, dark and towering. It was impossible to miss; if we got lost inside the border, we just needed to walk toward it.

Suddenly I froze, fear gripped my chest and my throat, and I had a difficult time breathing. We had been discovered. There was a soldier with a dog standing straight in front of us.

"Oh, God, we have been discovered, now we will be killed," I whispered to Mustafa. He was like a frozen statue, too. He stared hard but said he could not see anything. So this is how we die, this is the end of our short lives, I thought. I wasn't sure if they had seen us, but I threw myself to the ground and Mustafa followed. We hid in the grass, which stood pretty tall there.

We lay there for a few minutes, but it felt like an eternity to me. There was no motion from the soldier with the dog. I needed to see what they were doing so I raised my head just above the grass and stared toward them. They hadn't moved at all. I looked harder and slowly realized what I was seeing was a rock and bush. There was no soldier or dog. One moment before I had felt like crying, now I felt like laughing. My imagination was playing games with me. The relief from the tension was sudden and I could breathe easily again.

"There was no soldier with a dog," I said, grinning.

"Osman, let's walk," Mustafa reminded me, and we started walking. We kept the high mountain peak in sight and walked toward it. I walked fast — somewhere ahead was Greece, and freedom waiting to be discovered. We were excited and the emotion of fear was mixed with that of hope for our first taste of freedom. We saw a long, deep ditch and I walked toward it and then inside it. I knew I was getting closes to the second fence, but I could not see it from the ditch. I wondered whether I was ever going to make it to the other side. It felt as if we had been walking in no man's land forever. Finally, I was relieved to see the second fence in front of me.

Then all hell broke loose.

We heard the noise of the border guard jeeps. Somehow, they had managed to spot us. Not long after, I heard the voices of the guards yelling at us to stop or they would shoot. Before we understood what was going on, the loud boom of machine guns shattered the quiet night. I could hear the whistle of bullets flying pass our heads. We didn't have time to be horrified, we had to go or face imminent death. They were getting closer to us. I increased my speed and Mustafa was just behind me. Then the most dreadful thing happened, a moment I will never forget. It will haunt my dreams and memories for the rest of my life. I saw the second fence and had almost reached it when I heard loud machine gun fire and Mustafa collapsed on top of me. I was knocked down to the ground, which probably saved my life, because the loud machine gun fire continued. I extended my hand toward Mustafa's back and touched him and I felt my hand covered with warm liquid. The odor of the blood was like wet metal. I knew my best friend from my childhood had just been shot in the back. I was frantic.

"Mustafa! Mustafa, let's go to Greece, we are almost there!"

Then Mustafa said, with very soft words I could barely understand, "Brother, you go ...." Those were the last words that came from his mouth. I checked for breath and pulse, the way we were taught as children. No breath, no pulse. Mustafa was dead. How was this possible, I agonized, he was fine just a minute ago. Mustafa could not be dead. I didn't know whether I was saying or thinking those words. I know I started to cry silently, the tears blurred my vision, and I was ready to give up. Then I realized that it was strangely silent again. The border guards had lost sight of us when we had tumbled to the ground.

"Brother, you go."

I heard it again and again in my head and I realized that I was next to the barbed wire. Everything now looked hostile, small bushes and trees resembled border guards. I had to go, I had to push myself and remind myself that no good thing was waiting for me back there. Twenty or thirty feet past this barbed wire was Greece.

I crawled on the ground to the fence, got my small wire cutter from my pocket and started cutting the wire as fast as I could. My hands shook. I cut two lines, which was enough. I crawled under the fence frantically and I was on the other side. But I knew that I was still not safe and I continued to crawl. The guards still did not have sight of us; their strong flashlights cut the darkness in all directions, but not toward me. I had to make it to the woods. They were close, but I was still in an open field between the fence and the trees. I heard the voices of the guards approaching and that propelled me forward, crawling faster and faster. When I saw that the trees were really close, I got up and ran, bent over the way I had seen people run in the movies during battles. I was almost at the woods when I was spotted by the flashlights and immediately there was machine gun fire. I heard the bullets flying by my head and hitting the trees. I threw myself on the ground and crawled, touched the first tree in front of me, and threw myself behind it. I thought that this must be Greece, because there were woods again. There had been no trees inside no man's land, so this had to be the Greek part of the Rhodope Mountains. I could not relax yet. I remembered hearing a story about Bulgarian border guards crossing to the Greek side, killing defectors and dragging their bodies back to Bulgarian territory. When I got into the woods, I rose to my feet and ran as fast as I could. I knew I made it because the voices of the guards were a considerable distance away and I could hear them less and less. Nevertheless, I continued to run.

It was a cold night in the mountains, yet I was sweating profusely. I slowed down and walked briskly for ten, maybe twenty minutes. I was scared. I hunkered down in the woods and waited.

Finally the dawn broke slowly. I could see the green Rhodope Mountains on the Greek side and I thought how beautiful it was there. Then I heard the noise of trucks approaching and I saw Jeeps with Greek soldiers. They went toward the border and then they stopped. Loud commands were given to the solders in language I could not comprehend and I knew for sure that I was in Greece. I wondered if I should surrender to the soldiers, but with the memories fresh from last night's shooting, I was afraid, so I ran further into Greece.

Chapter 14

I had heard stories from my father and grandfather, talking about the small villages south of us in Greece, populated with Turks and Pomaks. I thought that if I could make it to one of those villages, the people there could help me to surrender to the local police or military border guards.

I walked at least for one hour in thick mountain forest. I did not see any border installations on the Greek side. Finally, I saw a narrow mountain road and I started following it. After about thirty minutes across a big hill I saw a small village similar to villages from the Bulgarian side of the border, with the roofs covered with flat stones. Perhaps this was a Turkish or Pomak village my father and grandfather had spoken of.

I didn't dare to go straight into the village. I sat and pondered what to do and decided to wait until later in the morning, because I thought that the villagers might be in better spirits and more helpful if they were not jolted out of sleep. As the sun rose in the sky, I gathered all my courage and headed for the village. I knocked on the door of one of the larger houses.

A man in his fifties appeared and I immediately pointed north, said "Bulgaria," and lifted my hands as if I was surrendering. It seemed that he was able to understand what I meant. He made a sign like "follow me." After about half an hour's walk, I was led to a small military border garrison. I saw the Greek flag and there was no longer any doubt in me that I was in Greece. I was in a free land. I was going to become a political refugee. The man said something to a soldier who looked at me, lifted his gun, and pointed for me to walk inside the border garrison. I was in the custody of the Greek border military.

That same day I was transferred to a small town, Komotini, south of the Bulgarian Greek border. The next day I was transferred to a big city, Thessaloniki. I was held in a cell, alone, in a police station, and spent one night there.

The next morning, I was taken to an office in the same building. Here, for the first time, I was questioned by a police officer who spoke good Bulgarian. He was medium build, olive-skinned with black hair. He was dressed in a nice police or military uniform. I could not distinguish which since I did not have any knowledge of Greek military or police. He was pleasant; he smiled and pointed to the chair opposite him.

"Welcome to Greece. How are you today?" he asked politely.

"I am well, thank you," I said.

"What is your name and date of birth?"

I told him.

"So could you tell me, why did you escape from Bulgaria?"

I was glad that he asked this question and I immediately responded.

"The Bulgarian police and military under the command of Bulgarian Communist Party are changing the names of Turks in Bulgaria at gunpoint. I did not want to spend the rest of my life in a country where the people are suppressed in such a vicious manner." I didn't mention anything about my assault on the zapastniak. I was afraid that it would constitute a reason for them to return me to the Bulgarian authorities.

He asked me to tell him in detail about what was going on in Bulgaria. I told him about the name change campaign, that it had been going pretty much all of 1984, but it had intensified in the fall and soon probably the names of all Turks living in southern Bulgaria would be changed.

"Why do you think the Bulgarian Communist Party is doing this?"

"They want to increase the numbers of Bulgarians in the country," I responded right away.

"What other reasons do you think that there are for these events of the name change campaign?"

I had heard an opinion on Radio Free Europe, one I agreed with, so I said, "They view the Turkish minority as a serious threat to the Communist system."

"Why do you think so?"

"The Bulgarian government thinks Turks in Bulgaria are related to the Turks in Turkey, so they would never fight their fellow Turks who are members of Western NATO. Bulgaria is a member of the Communist Warsaw Pact."

"Can you think of other reasons they are doing this?"

"The party leaders claim that the Turks want autonomy within Bulgaria, which is a lie being fed to the Bulgarian population, so the Bulgarians support the party in this crime against humanity." I had heard the statement "crime against humanity" on Radio Free Europe. I thought the statement truthfully reflected the situation of the Turks living in Bulgaria.

The officer again looked me in the eye and asked, "If we decide to return you to Bulgarian authorities, what do you think will happen to you?"

"I will face death or a long prison term or even a death camp," I said solemnly.

"If we let you go anywhere in the world, where would you like to go?"

"Turkey," I said immediately.

"Our relations with Turkey are not that good at the present time," the officer said, after a moment of contemplation. "It could take you years to obtain a visa for Turkey, but only a few months to get a visa to America. First, you will need to apply to the United Nations High Commissioner of Refugees for refugee status. Their representative will visit you in the camp."

There was no way for me to know whether the officer was completely sincere about the Turkish visa. I wondered why the Turkish embassy would not issue a visa to a Turk from Bulgaria who was escaping violent suppression, as long as I was allowed by the Greek government to apply for the visa.

"If I cannot go to Turkey, then I would like to go to America. But, I would like to have time to contemplate this issue. All these events are happening too fast," I said.

"You will have enough time to think about this issue in the Lavrion refugee camp. You will be moved there tomorrow. Good luck to you." The officer got up, and I guessed that meant the questioning was over so I got up, too.

A police guard showed me the way back to my cell.

The next day, early in the morning, I was awakened and ordered to get ready. I was put in a police Jeep and driven to Athens, where I was transferred to a different vehicle that took me to the Lavrion refugee camp.

After a week in the refugee camp, as the Greek agent had promised, I was visited by the representative of the United Nations High Commissioner of Refugees. He was a serious, middle-aged, graying man in a grey suit, white shirt, and blue tie. He gave me forms to fill out in Bulgarian and I had a lengthy interview about the circumstances of my escape from Bulgaria and the name change campaign conducted there.

"We have lots of information from the foreign diplomats stationed in Bulgaria which support your story," he said at the end. "I am positive that you will be given refugee status which will open your way to apply to the U.S. embassy for asylum. Most likely a representative of the U.S. Immigration and Naturalization Service will come to visit you and you will have to fill out an application with them."

Then the long and nerve-wracking process for getting the refugee status began. After many months of waiting, finally I got the visa and I was set to travel to the United States.

Chapter 15

I was impressed by what I saw upon my arrival in Chicago. When the airplane was descending for landing at O'Hare International Airport after the long flight from Athens, the city lights were like endless stars in the sky. It was difficult for me to believe that all those lights were electric lights, because never in my life had I seen so many. I was a peasant boy from a dark village in the heart of the Balkans. I thought all those city lights were the stars reflected on the surface of Lake Michigan, which I knew about from my geography class. In a way, I was like the natives from the Caribbean Islands who could not see Christopher Columbus' armada, because they didn't have previous knowledge of the existence of ships. It was explained to them by the shaman that the ships were there and after that they were able to see them.

When the airplane got really close to the land, it dawned on me that I wasn't seeing the stars, those were real electric lights. I was dumbstruck by the sea of never-ending lights and the sheer size of the city. I guess our eyes refuse to see what the mind does not know.

Arriving in America was intimidating, especially if you didn't know anybody in the country. It was easy to feel utterly lost and alone in the sea of people at the airport. When we disembarked and went to customs, I presented my papers to the customs officer.

"Welcome to America," he said, smiling.

This "Welcome to America" after so many years still rings in my ears. The customs officer told me what to do to get my status in order and be released.

While my documents were being processed, I was assigned a Bulgarian translator. I was stunned that this young and pretty American lady spoke Bulgarian fluently. Later, during our conversation, I found out that she was actually Bulgarian.

"What is going on in Bulgaria?" she asked. I thought I detected sadness in her voice and eyes. Maybe, I thought, she was homesick.

"Unfortunately, the Communists are ruling Bulgaria with an iron fist," I replied.

After my papers were processed, I met with an officer of the Immigration and Naturalization Service who issued my green card and told me that I had the right to reside and work in the U.S. indefinitely. Holding my precious papers close to my chest, I exited the customs office and went to the arrivals terminal where there were many people exiting and even more people waiting for their loved ones. I felt like an animal freed after being kept in a cage for too long. I was not sure what to do, how to act, or what to expect. I looked left and right and I was stunned to see a small group right in the front of the wide exit door, holding a fairly big sign with the name "Osman" on it. Were these people waiting for me? Maybe they were waiting for a different Osman. I knew from the refugee camp in Lavrion that I was going to be met by the members of the political asylum group, but I could not make myself believe that these people were really waiting for me. My curiosity prevailed and I walked toward the group. As I approached, they all looked toward me, probably because my ragtag clothing, the latest fashion of advanced socialism, made such an impression on them. I wanted to find out whom they were waiting for without attracting too much attention, but at that point it was too late. I approached the group slowly and pointed at the sign and then pointed toward myself and said Osman. They all smiled and started talking among themselves excitedly. Then one of the ladies approached me and extended her hand. I took it and we shook hands. She pointed toward herself and said slowly, "My name is Maria."

"Osman, Osman. I am a refugee from Bulgaria," I said, still shaking her hand.

These people were members of the Christian Church asylum committee for refugees, who were my sponsors. All of them smiled warmly and each shook my hand. They had been waiting for me, I was somebody, in their estimation. At that moment I felt less intimidated arriving in America alone. These people were here to help me. Maria was a nice lady in her forties. She was dressed simply, with jeans and a nice, bright blue shirt. She had short, blond hair and blue eyes. She looked like a simple woman with an unforced, natural smile and twinkle in her eyes. Later, I would learn that Maria was a devoted Christian. The rest of the group consisted of two women and one man, all in their forties and fifties, all very nice and all said, "Welcome to America." I managed to muster a thank you from what I had learned from the Voice of America lessons, the little bit of studying I had done in Bulgaria, and the refugee camp in Lavrion. They paid for a small room for me free of charge since I did not have any money. I was happy and grateful for the help of the asylum committee. I went through a short period of euphoria, because I had made it to America. I wanted to experience and see as much as possible, but after a few days I could not help but think about my family, my beloved Leyla, and my friend Mustafa's family. I was wandering whether Mustafa's parents knew what had happened to their son.

I would spend long sleepless nights thinking about all of them.

$$* \qquad * \qquad *$$

I had been taking care of the sheep and goats, and I was leading them to pasture up by the hills situated behind the village. It was a lovely, early summer day with the almond and linden trees blooming and filling the air with lovely aromas. I was bathed in the sun's warm and brilliant light. The colors of the village were vibrant. With short calls, I encouraged the flock to move toward the pasture. They knew what I wanted and they would move when I called to them. I was past the village, walking toward the hills when I saw a big person in a dark cloak approaching me and he held something in his hand. In the beginning I was puzzled as to what he wanted, then I saw the bright light and thunder coming from the machine gun he was holding in his hands. I realized that the man was a border guard and he was shooting at me. I was scared beyond words and started to run, but I could not run fast enough. It was like moving in slow motion and even my scream came slowly from my chest. In an instant I realized that I had been shot and blood squirted out of the wounds in my arm and abdomen. I wanted to keep running, but I felt that my legs were betraying me, they turned soft and unresponsive and, despite my wildest desire, I slowly but inevitably collapsed to the ground. I could see the face of the attacker, contorted in a hateful grimace, looking half-wolf, half-human, with big and sharp wolf-like fangs. He approached me and sank his sharp teeth into the bleeding wound on my arm and started drinking my blood. I was frightened to death.

I would wake up from this dreadful dream screaming at the top of my lungs in terror, struggling to breathe, as if I was drowning, because there was not enough oxygen in the air.

I had variations of this dream, of being chased by a border guard, night after night for months after my arrival in America. It felt like forever before the terror started to diminish.

I was homesick and lovesick, and in my daydreams I often entertained the idea of going back and visiting my family and Leyla. But I knew that I could not go back to Bulgaria legally. I would have to slip through the border again, in and out. I knew that this time I would not have a friend who would take a bullet for me, yet I was willing to put my life on the line just so I could see my beloved Leyla and my family one more time. If love was not worth dying for, then what was the purpose of a life lived lonely, like a shadow?

I thought that I could not live without seeing them again. It was difficult to realize that this was just a daydream, but I needed it, it was part of me, it made me feel alive and gave me some purpose to live for.

I took care of myself, dressed and went to work and school, but that nagging homesickness and the horrifying dreams were always there. In the beginning I thought that I would not make it, I would not survive, so strong was the grip of homesickness and so horrifying the dreams. The feeling of homesickness would be like a black stone on my chest for years. After a while I realized that if kept myself busy and distracted, I felt it less. Interacting with the members of the asylum committee helped enormously. When I improved my English and I was able to hold a basic conversation, I went and talked to them and I felt the enormous burden, pain and weight of homesickness lifting off my shoulders, at least temporarily. I would talk in broken English, feeling the pain ease.

Those first few months I also thought of the people I had left behind. What would happen to them, my beloved Leyla, my family, my village and all the Turks of Bulgaria? I could not foresee that within a few short years, the Communist bloc would collapse and one of the factors of the collapse of the regime in Bulgaria was the continual peaceful resistance of the Turks of Bulgaria. When I was in Bulgaria, the leaders of the Bulgarian Communist Party preached that Communism would prevail everywhere, it would never fail. They probably wanted to reassure themselves.

One day I was helping Maria fold and store clothing that the asylum committee collected for refugees, when I voiced the question that had been turning in my head for a while now.

"Why did I have to be the one to end up separated from my Leyla, my parents, the people I cared about?"

Maria lifted her head and looked at me with her clear blue eyes. She thought for a moment and adjusted her eyeglasses by pushing them back toward her eyes.

"We need people like you who rebel against the Communist regime," she said. "If there were not people like you who managed to escape from Communist repression, how we would know what was really happening there? You have a special mission, you are a messenger of truth. We believe you and everybody who hears your story believes you, because you came from there."

Just like that, Maria managed to lift my spirits. I began to feel better about myself and I thought that Maria was right and I had an obligation to tell the truth about the plight of the Turks in Bulgaria. Slowly I realized that I didn't have to be a victim. I knew that my thoughts and feelings would not change overnight, but Maria's words made me feel better about myself, my environment, and my life. After all, maybe I had a say in my life. I didn't want my future to be defined by my past, I didn't want to be held hostage by my past. I could better my life by applying myself to my studies to change my life for the better.

Chapter 16

I decided I would get a degree from college in the hope of being useful to the people around me and my family back at home. But first I needed to learn English. I enrolled in the English as a Second Language, ESL, class in the local college with the help of my new friends from the asylum committee. There I met my professor of English language and literature, Peter Williams.

He thought that America should be liked and admired, not only for the prosperity and economic opportunities that it offered, but also because of its democracy and freedom. Professor Williams was genuinely interested in the stories of his students. He taught a large group of international students and new citizens. He wanted to know what had caused them to leave their countries.

He asked what brought me here. I told him I had escaped from the oppression and tyranny of the Communist system in Bulgaria, and I explained the name change campaign. He was genuinely intrigued by my escape and stories of the Turks in Bulgaria and life behind the Iron Curtain.

"This was such a shocking violation of human rights," he said after one of his classes. "I am sure there are many Bulgarians, along with the Turks, who feel oppressed and want regime change, too. What do you think, Osman? How do you think this problem can be solved?"

"At this point I don't have a clear idea, but the destruction of the Communist regime would help," I said.

"If the Communist regime, or if the regime that comes after the Communists, is reluctant to tackle the problem of the renaming of the Turks, what do you think can be done to solve the problem?"

"I really never thought that far," I said, with genuine puzzlement. It was a valid question.

"It seems this problem was a fight for more than just basic rights," Professor Williams said. "There are nationalistic feelings running high at this time, on both sides by now, and that will make the solution of the problem difficult."

"I completely agree and I see that you comprehend this issue well," I said. "We, the common Turks, have always been able to live peacefully with our Bulgarian neighbors. I don't see why we can't do that in the future."

Professor Williams looked at me with an enigmatic expression on his face.

"If, say, the Communists are defeated in Bulgaria and the next government is democratically elected, but still refuses to reinstate the names and rights of the Turks, what do you think the solution should be?"

I was not sure how to respond. "I have no clear idea," I said slowly, "but I am thinking we will continue to fight for our rights until they are reinstated. Also, any Bulgarian government which refuses to reinstate the rights of Turks should have to face the wrath of about one million of its citizens. I don't think the Turks will stop the fight for their rights until they get them back, and this time we probably will be looking for the Bulgarian government to guarantee our rights in the Bulgarian constitution."

"True democracy for Bulgaria will gradually solve the poblem," Professor Williams said. "It is not a magic bullet though, but it is the closest we can get to one. I don't think rulers can sustain this internal tension, international condemnation, and isolation indefinitely. so they will be forced to deal with the problem." I thought about what Professor Williams said for a moment.

"It was a long shot," I said, "but it can be achieved. But the whole Bulgarian population has to change their way of thinking about politics."

Professor Williams thought that people in other countries had intelligence to solve their own problems. He definitely was for education and recognizing any potential adversary to our way of thinking. He thought that the pen was mightier than the sword, and that we should use any means necessary to change the minds and win the hearts of our foe. He thought that we would not be able to control our adversaries by trying physically to destroy them; we should try to change their way of thinking.

Toward the end of the first year of college, Professor Williams sought me out, smiling.

"Osman, I have a favor to ask of you."

"What can I do for you, sir?" I asked, intrigued.

"We will be having the graduation ceremony in May. I need somebody to carry the American flag. Do you think that you are up to the task?"

I was surprised that, from so many students, he picked me, but I did not hesitate.

"It would be a great honor for me to carry the flag," I said. "I am humbled by your request. I will be happy to do it."

The commencement day arrived quickly and the air was festive filled with excitement. Everybody was dressed up, happy and upbeat. I was dressed in a nice pair of black pants and a pressed white shirt. I was so honored that Professor Williams had chosen me to carry the flag.

I felt like I was flying while performing my duties. A tremendous energy and courage coursed through me like electrical current. The stadium where the commencement ceremony was going to be held was washed in the brightest sunlight that afternoon. There was an enormous crowd of parents, relatives, and friends of the graduating students there to witness the ceremony. I was proud that from all the American students, I, a humble Turk from Bulgaria, had the honor of carrying Old Glory.

In 1985, the year I arrived in America, Ronald Reagan was sworn in for a second term of office. Something else very important also happened in the Soviet Union in March of 1985. Mikhail Gorbachev was named the new leader. The political decisions of Gorbachev would have a positive impact on Bulgarian politics. They would hasten the fall of Communism, and facilitate a march for freedom for all people living under the yoke of Communism, who hoped to soon experience the same right to choose their own path in life the way I was here in my new home.

Chapter 17

One day the gracious Maria introduced me to Metin Arman, a Turk from Bulgaria. Metin smiled at me and firmly shook my hand while saying, "Welcome to America, Osman." He hugged me in a warm friendly manner, customary among Turks back home.

He was a medium build, strong man in his late forties. He was dressed in a nice suit. He had escaped from Bulgaria thirty years ago when he was sixteen years old after the Bulgarian Communists killed his parents in the process of nationalizing their land. He thought that there was no life for him in Bulgaria and just walked to Greece, which was not that far from his village.

The border was not guarded that strictly at the time. Communists were just establishing themselves in the country with the "help" of the Soviets and had not yet erected the elaborate border fence. Of course, the Soviets would soon be "teaching" the Bulgarian Communists how to build a totalitarian regime and how to erect the Iron Curtain. By this time the Soviets had considerable experience in building totalitarian regimes, iron-clad borders and the wholesale murder of innocent people. This whole horrible process was put into practice against the people who wanted real democracy in Bulgaria and the ethnic minorities. All who dared to express a view differing from the Party line were dealt with most severely; most of the time they met their end.

Metin was president of the Chicago branch of the Solidarity of Balkan Turks of America. Most of the members of this organization were Turks from Bulgaria.

"A few days ago Maria contacted me over the phone and told me that you escaped Bulgaria and have been living here for a while," Metin said. "There are other Turks from Bulgaria living here and we meet and discuss the situation back home. We are well informed about the events of the horrible name change campaign against the Turks. The American people and government will do everything possible to assist the repressed Turks of Communist Bulgaria." It was nice that he had knowledge of events occurring very far away, behind the Iron Curtain, where the Communist regime did everything possible to hide the truth.

"Osman, the issue of forceful assimilation of the Turks of Bulgaria will be resolved in favor of the Turks. I don't want you to doubt that even for a moment," he said with unshakable belief and confidence.

I admired his optimism, but I was astonished that Metin believed this. But that was Metin — perpetual optimist, true leader.

"I really would like to believe you," I said, "but I think that is a very strong statement to say, considering the fact that Communism is still very strong and there are no signs that the Bulgarian Communist Party leaders will change their stance on assimilation any time soon. On the contrary, the Bulgarian Communist Party is releasing statement after statement that there are no Turks in Bulgaria. They are never going to change their stance on this issue."

I never had had the opportunity to rub shoulders with men like Metin before, partly because I had come from behind the Iron Curtain, where free and independent thinkers and entrepreneurs were not tolerated by the Communist regime. I realized that I needed to change my thinking to be more in line with Metin's.

I shared my amazement of the nice buildings and the huge stores with abundance of merchandise. He said that he could appreciate my view, he was like me when he first arrived in America years earlier.

"Your fresh view of America, of an outsider, helps me see again how rich and wealthy this country is, and the opportunities for enterprising minds are virtually limitless."

I visited Metin's family in their nice home in a Chicago suburb. The house was two stories with many rooms, and was surrounded with mowed green lawn. I was impressed with the interior of the house, the big living room, large TV and a comfortable sofa and chairs. I liked the hot running water in the bathroom and big bathtub. Until that day, I had seen bathtubs only in the movies. Central heating and air conditioning was something new and amazing, to be able to control heat and cool air with the single push of a button.

Metin came to America with nothing except the clothing on his back. He had escaped to Greece one dark, cold fall night, all by himself. A church in a small Midwestern town situated near Chicago sponsored Metin and he was able to travel to America just before Christmas.

At the beginning, people from the church helped him find a place to stay, a job, and helped him learn English. In the small town, Metin felt lonely and homesick. He wanted to move to the big city where there were better job and business opportunities. He wanted to study and accomplish something during his lifetime. After almost year, he moved to Chicago, studying during the day at a high school and working during the evenings to support himself. He gradually found from experience and study that America was the country of unlimited opportunities for enterprising people. He heard and read about countless success stories of people who had come to America and worked hard and had succeeded. Metin had enthusiasm and the intense desire and drive to succeed.

In Chicago, Metin was able to get in touch with the Turks from Bulgaria through the small organization called Solidarity of Balkan Turks of America, where he met his future father-in-law, Rasim. Rasim liked Metin's energy and enthusiasm for life in America, and he offered him a job at his gas station which he owned and operated. There Metin met the beautiful and intelligent Aysel, Rasim's daughter. Metin and Aysel liked each other from the very beginning and worked together in running the gas station. After less than year they were married.

Metin wanted to succeed in a real estate business. He read many books and attended seminars to acquire information on how to build and run such a business. He scouted places, searching for apartment blocks that he could buy, fix, and rent for profit. He found a place in Aurora, Illinois, and offered Rasim a partnership. Rasim would supply the capital, and Metin would fix the apartments and find tenants for them. After some consideration, Rasim agreed. That's how Metin started. By the time I met him, Metin owned hundreds of rental apartments in the Chicago area. He had achieved his dream and continued to expand and grow his business. Later, he started building houses and selling them and became a real estate developer.

Since our lives are inevitably affected by the people with whom we associate, Metin managed to install this positive impression of America in me, not only with his words, but also by his deeds. By building houses, he was contributing to the country's wealth.

Metin thought that I should go back to school, because school was essential for success in America. First, I got a small apartment not far from Metin's house and the community college which I was going to attend. In the following few years, I had to study hard and I worked part-time as a porter in a department store. Often Metin would invite me to spend time with his family on the weekends. He would often repeat that Communist countries didn't have a chance against America, in the arms race or any other race. He was sure beyond the shadow of a doubt that soon or later the evil empire of the Communist Bloc would crumble. I think that he believed what Ronald Reagan said about Communism: "The West will not contain Communism, it will transcend Communism. We will not bother to denounce it, we'll dismiss it as a sad, bizarre chapter in human history whose last pages are even now being written."

Initially, I was intimidated by the size of the city and crowds on the street of downtown Chicago, but gradually I got used to the perpetual hurry and energy. Metin would take me for drives downtown and show me the buildings in his brand new 1985 maroon Cadillac Eldorado Biarritz, which he referred to as his working car. I thought it was the coolest car in the world. I could barely hear the engine and it moved so smoothly I had the feeling that the car was not touching the road; it felt as if it was hovering. I have to admit that when we first went sightseeing in downtown Chicago, I was intimidated by the huge skyscrapers. I was shocked by the size of the buildings. When I visited the sky deck of the Sears Tower for the first time with Metin, I was very impressed. The view from the tower was like nothing I have ever seen or experienced before. The perfect rectangular grid of downtown was simply unbelievable. There, I thought to myself, why wouldn't people want to come to America? Was there anything more impressive or larger than this anywhere else in the world?

When I visited the Art Institute of Chicago for the first time I entered a gallery featuring French painters. I immediately recognized the painting by French painter George-Pierre Seurat, *A Sunday on La Grande Jatte* from my *Hristomatia*, my book with excerpts from great works of world literature and photos of great paintings of Western Renaissance and some Bulgarian painters. When I was back in Bulgaria, I knew all these great paintings existed somewhere far away in French or American art galleries, but I thought I never would be able to see them in person. Yet I stood right there, in the front of the great painting. This was not a reproduction. No, this was the original, painted by a great French artist.

What a great place this art gallery was, I thought. It was the perfect place to relax and soak up culture after a long, hard work week. There was only one person in my mind — my enchanting Leyla. When I got very homesick and lonely, I would go to the art institute and look at that painting, along with others, which calmed and uplifted my spirit.

*   *   *

In Chicago, I also loved Grand Park; I liked to sit on one of the benches and rest my eyes on its Buckingham Fountain. This place was so well maintained and clean. People came and went, mostly visitors from other parts of the country, and many foreigners. They took pictures, preserving their own images and memories of the fountain. When the weather was nice, there was no place like the park, the skyline in the background was simply breathtaking. This was Chicago, my new home — not bad at all.

It was a clear, warm spring day. I sat and tried not to think of anything. To a certain extent, I was tired of thinking, tired of worrying about the people I had left behind, tired of thinking about my future. Going through ups and downs, I sometimes had a difficult time enjoying myself in the present. But that day, my mind decided that it had had enough and needed to rest. I was sitting there on the bench and soaking up the warm sun rays of the spring — nothing like it after a long, cold winter.

Then my eyelids got heavier and heavier. I didn't know whether I was dreaming or having a vision. It was not like dreams I experienced before. I knew that I was sitting there on the bench, but then I saw my hands dissolving in the air as sugar dissolves in water. Then my arms, my feet, and legs dissolved and I was on the border of the Iron Curtain. I saw the guard approaching with a gun pointed at me; he lifted his machine gun at me and started shooting at close range. Yet somehow I was unfazed — they could not hurt me, their bullets flew through me as if I were not there. Then my whole body dissolved. I smiled at the guards and thought, How can you kill me when I don't exist in your world? I smiled, I laughed, I didn't exist, but I was unfazed, unafraid. On the contrary, I was calm; there was peace in me and in the universe. Why should I worry about anything if I didn't exist. Then I slowly opened my eyes and I was there, on the bench in Grand Park, looking at Buckingham Fountain. I felt refreshed and hopeful. A dream or a vision, I was not sure, but, as the song goes, "I Feel Good."

Chapter 18

I had to work hard, study hard, and learn a new language. I had no doubt that I would better my life, as the opportunities in this great country were plentiful. I did suffer in the beginning from terrible homesickness, having never in my life been away from home and that simple life. I dreamed every night that I was back home with my parents, or that Leyla was asking me to come back to her. The dreams with Leyla were so vivid they felt more real than life itself. In the dreams, I was so happy with her, but very often there would be this huge black dog that reminded me so much of the German Shepherd border dogs, which were trained to chase and apprehend defectors from Bulgaria. The dog would come in between us, I would awaken in sheer terror and wonder where I was for a minute or two before realizing the painful truth that I was alone.

I did not know that with the passage of time, these homesickness pangs would lessen and fade away, and one day I would feel as comfortable in America as I had been in my village. But such a day was far away, and it felt as if it would never come. The mental anguish was turning to physical pain. My stomach would tighten along with many other muscles in my body, and I would feel an aching in the bottom of my stomach. Time slowed time down and my distress would get worse. There was no escape from the homesickness; it was inside of me and there was nothing I could do to get rid of it. There was no chance I would ever be reunited with the girl I still loved so much. We were separated by the Iron Curtain and Communism was standing between us strong, like that dark, evil dog from my dream.

I studied hard. I knew that knowing and understanding English was key to success in America. Step by step, word by word, a new world was opening in front of my eyes, the world of the English language. I was excited to be able to understand words and sentences in magazine and newspaper articles. The fact that I understood the meaning of sentences or the whole article motivated me to first use it and then expand my knowledge by learning more and more. I was also motivated to learn because I wanted to know what was going on with the people in Eastern Europe and the Turkish minority in Bulgaria. In order to learn, I would wander into libraries where I would spend a great deal of time deciphering English.

During the weekend, when I had time to myself, I would drive my old Monte Carlo to the park and spend quiet time alone, enjoying the stillness and quiet of the night. I connected with nature and remembered the fragrant smell of the almond and linden trees blooming during the spring back at home, and lying on the fragrant alfalfa and the stillness and beauty of the night sky, which I missed seeing in the city. I could not forget Mustafa, whose life was so brutally ended at the border. I thought of Leyla and my parents and sadness would slowly crawl in. I would feel this increasing heaviness on my chest and breathing would become difficult. I thought about what we would be doing if Mustafa were still alive and I was back in my village. Homesickness was excruciatingly painful. It was a heavy stone on my shoulders, dragging me down. I knew I needed to put my past behind me and live in the present, but it was not so easy to let go. Life is not like a book where you can just turn to a new page on a whim.

I would read in the newspaper about the old Communist rhetoric, that they would have the ultimate victory. I knew that the people in power would never give up voluntarily. They had perfected their system of suppression and brain washing, but there were cracks in their system and things were changing in Eastern Europe. People were not willing to stand by passively anymore — they wanted change. I knew that Turks of Bulgaria wanted that change most desperately, because they were some of the most suppressed people of Eastern Europe. I knew that the resentment and hatred against the regime was growing every day and would soon explode in the unstoppable rage of the masses, but I did not know when and how all this would materialize. I had doubts and fears that, if there were a spontaneous uprising against the regime, countless innocent people would be killed mercilessly by those in power. I was praying that the changes would happen in a peaceful manner. Not much changed in Bulgaria between 1985 and 1989, however, except for the occasional defector who would arrive and tell us that the government was continuing to oppress all the people in Bulgaria, and Turks of Bulgaria were the most oppressed of all of them.

I vividly remember the speech given by President Ronald Reagan June 12, 1987, in front of the Berlin Wall in West Germany, and him saying "Mr. Gorbachev, tear down this wall!" This speech brought joy and immense hope to my heart. Maybe now there was hope for the people of Eastern Europe.

The year of 1989 seemed like any other — no great changes, no great expectations for the people of Eastern Europe. Underneath the seemingly calm surface of life there, however, powerful forces were gathering. Soon lots of things were happening again in Eastern Europe. Gorbachev was still in power in the Soviet Union, and his reluctance to use military power to subdue the movements for freedom probably saved the lives of countless people. Germans were fleeing East Germany in hordes, through Hungary to Austria. There were articles in *The Chicago Tribune* describing the violence of the Bulgarian Communist government against the peaceful Turks, whose great discontentment would lead to a series of peaceful demonstrations in southern and northern Bulgaria in May of 1989. These demonstrations were violently suppressed by the Bulgarian police and military, and many demonstrators were killed. The Bulgarian Communist regime saw no way out of the situation. The pressure on all sides was rising, and the rulers were aware of it, realizing the name change campaign was going nowhere. There was only one thing they could do to avoid further escalation of the tension — they had to open the borders for the restless Turkish minority, let them go, and decrease the political pressure inside the country.

I remember reading about the demonstrations and the killings of Turks in the local newspaper. I could not believe my eyes when I read about the expulsion of the first Turks from Bulgaria to Austria and Yugoslavia. By the end of May, the Bulgarian government started issuing passports to the Turks and in the beginning, forcing them to go to Turkey, after which a huge flood of Turks from Bulgaria to Turkey followed. All through June, we watched on television as the Turks moved.

I wished to be reunited with my family I missed so dearly. Also, I wished desperately to be reunited with Leyla. I had kept my memories of Leyla alive for five long years, as the Iron Curtain prohibited communication, repeatedly thinking of her and our encounters. I needed to put my past behind me, but I was too close in time to my past. I needed to come to terms with the guilt which had been a part of me since that fateful night at the border when Mustafa took a bullet for me. I was the reason Mustafa was on the border that dreadful night. I needed to go back and face Mustafa's parents and let them tell me who they thought was guilty for their son's death. I needed to tell them that their son saved my life, just by being there. I could not go on living like this, in endless suffering, under this heavy burden of guilt. I had not been able to go back to Bulgaria for almost five years, but now it seemed that things were going to change for the good. I knew how unyielding the Communists could be, and the change in their stand was shocking to me.

I did not know whether my family was in Bulgaria or Turkey. I did not know where they intended to live or stay or when or if they were going to move. I did not have a way to contact them there since telephones had been shut down by the regime in Bulgaria. I was desperate and did not know what to do.

During conversation with Metin about the situation in Bulgaria, he suggested that I travel to Turkey and search for my family. He said that these were trying times for the Bulgarian Turks and it was my right to go and see my family. I had been through so much and had to overcome so much to get to this point in my life. All the obstacles made me stronger and motivated me to do better. The bigger the obstacles are, the bigger person you have the chance of becoming.

Chapter 19

In the summer of 1989 I was set to travel to Turkey for the first time in my life. Growing up, I had been told that I was a Turk, yet I had never been to Turkey. I did not know what to expect, but I was so excited that I could not sleep the night before the flight. People say that time heals a broken heart, but I felt that my love and longing for Leyla increased with the passage of time. I wanted to meet my family, but, deep in my heart, I was really hoping to be reunited with Leyla, the girl I loved more than anything. Most of my thoughts revolved around Leyla.

The newspaper articles and TV news said that the members of the Turkish minority who clashed with the police and military during the name change campaign were issued new passports first so they could move out of the country. I suspected that locating the refugees in Turkey would be difficult, if not impossible, because most of the people who moved didn't have a permanent address in Turkey. They moved from place to place. First, they would be sent to massive tented cities near the border city of Edirne; after that, some of them would be moved to schools which had been converted to living quarters for the summer of 1989. Many left there to be with their relatives. Those with relatives were the lucky ones because they were helped with finding work. Of course, the Turkish government helped, too, but it was overwhelmed with the great number of immigrants coming within such a short time frame.

With the help of the Turkish embassy in the U.S., I was able to get in touch with Zeynep, my aunt, who lived in Istanbul. Her family moved there in 1977 during the last organized emigration of Turks from Bulgaria. I wrote her a letter about the situation in Bulgaria. She replied, asking me to visit and meet her and the family in Turkey. Now was a good time for me to take advantage of her invitation. I had her telephone number, so I called her and let her know when I was arriving.

I boarded the big airplane at Chicago's O'Hare airport, my new American passport in hand. I had not used it before. After living as a political refugee in America for two years, I was eligible to become an American citizen. Metin suggested that it would be a good idea to get the American citizenship and passport, because he thought that things in Bulgaria would not always be unsettled, they would change and I might need to travel. Time showed he was right.

The flight from Chicago to Istanbul was about 10 hours long and tiring. It went through the night, and in the morning we were told that we were approaching Istanbul and would be landing shortly. I looked from the window and saw an endless sea of buildings. Istanbul's size defied imagination.

I didn't know whether I would be able to recognize my aunt, as my memories from my childhood were sketchy. I could remember one cold December day in 1977 when my father and mother embraced my aunt for the last time on the train station platform in Kardjali; all of them were crying. They were being separated and they didn't know for how long. I was hoping that my aunt would recognize me.

When I passed through customs and went to the gate, there were many people who were waiting for loved ones to arrive. I saw a woman with a colorful scarf on her head waving at me. She looked vaguely familiar.

"Selamun aleykum, Zeynep abla," Hello, I said, and as I was taught when I was young, I held her hand and kissed it.

"Aleykum selam," she said with a broad smile. "Osman, you look so much like your father. That was how I was able to immediately recognize you. I remember you as a small child, when I saw you for the last time in Kardjali train station. Look at you now — you are a grown man."

I went to kiss my Uncle Jafer's hand, too, but he grabbed me and gave me a big hug. He drove the small Turkish-made Murat to their house. The traffic on the street was chaotic; it felt as if they had more cars than their roads could handle. Their house was fairly big, two stories with spacious rooms, and it had a small yard only in the front. On both sides, it was connected or touching the neighbor's house.

I was invited into the living room, which was ornate with a nice chandelier and fine furniture. My aunt was barely middle class, but their house had a nice interior.

I sat on a fancy couch and my aunt quickly prepared tea. I would soon discover that all Turks living in Turkey drank lots of tea, and I would certainly have my share during my stay.

"I am hoping to meet my parents when they come to Turkey," I said. "I miss them very much."

"I heard that they are on their way," my aunt replied. "Finally, they will be saved from that evil Communist regime. I am so happy for them, and for you, too."

"I am not here to stay in Turkey," I said. "I would like to go back to the States and finish my studies."

"But of course, education is a very important thing, especially nowadays," she said earnestly, before sipping her tea.

"There was also somebody else I want to meet in Turkey," I said. "There was a girl, Leyla. I met her when I was in Bulgaria and I know she lives in Turkey. I have her relatives' address, and I am interested in finding her and re-establishing contact. I was sincerely thinking of marrying her."

"Of course, I would be delighted to help you," my aunt replied, smiling. "That is so sweet that you remember Leyla from so long ago. I will immediately talk to all the ladies who moved here from Bulgaria. I am happy to do it, we will find her."

I wanted to go and search for my parents and Leyla myself. My plan was simple — I would go to the border gate between Turkey and Bulgaria, Kapıkule, and ask people coming from Bulgaria about my family. I didn't know what else I could do to get in touch with my relatives or my neighbors from Çalıköy. The Turkish government officials were willing to help, but they had a difficult time tracking people because they were inundated with so many refugees.

My aunt told me that the Turks from Bulgaria were from all over the country. In the summer of 1989, thousands of people a day were moving to Turkey and the Turkish government had to feed them, house them temporarily, and later provide them with jobs and permanent houses. At one point, it just overwhelmed the country; there were too many people coming in too short a time. Looking for somebody and finding them in this chaotic stream of people was pretty much like finding a needle in a haystack. But I decided that I would take a chance and look for my family and Leyla anyway.

My aunt and uncle decided they would help me in any way they could. Jafer took Friday off from work and we drove to Edirne. When we approached the city, in the distance we could see the tent cities. There were huge spaces covered with probably thousands of tents. We saw the endless stream of Turks arriving from Bulgaria. The view was staggering, something that will stay with me for the rest of my life. Why did these people have to be uprooted from their place of birth in such a drastic manner? Why did these people have to be put through this inhumane suffering? These people were treated like nothing more than animals by the Communist regime in Bulgaria. At that point, I realized that it was one thing to see pictures and read about human suffering, but it was very different to experience it firsthand.

Chapter 20

The mosques and minarets made the city more Middle Eastern than European, but that was the great charm of Istanbul, that in a peaceful manner it embraced both cultures. The city was a fantastic mixture of eastern and western architecture, of old churches, mosques, houses, castles, great yalis, houses of noble Turks, many of them built during the late years of the Ottoman Empire. The sultans' palaces were among the most interesting places to visit, but the most famous building was the Hagia Sofia museum, which was situated on Sultan Ahmet Square.

The Hagia Sofia, an Eastern Orthodox Church, was built by the Byzantine Emperor Justinian. In A.D. 532, Emperor Justinian had ordered the massacre of thirty thousand soldiers who had rebelled against his rule. Justinian considered fleeing the city to avoid the fury of the rebels, but the strong and smart empress Theodora persuaded Justinian to stay put and fight. Justinian ordered his generals to gather the troops and massacre the rebels, even though most of the city was burned to the ground. The emperor saw the opportunity to rebuild the city, and he built one of the most magnificent churches of all time, the Hagia Sofia, completed in A.D. 537. When the church was damaged by earthquakes, it was said that the church would heal itself or the damage would miraculously fix itself. Later, when the Turks conquered Constantinople, they converted the church to a mosque. When the Turkish Republic was established by Mustafa Kemal Ataturk the mosque was turned to a museum.

I didn't have time or the mood, however, to enjoy all these wonders of the city. I was worried about my parents because I could not find any information about them, ever since I had arrived. The number of Turks from Bulgaria crossing the border had swelled to hundreds of thousands at this point, and it was extremely difficult to find anybody in such a huge crowd. The easiest way for anyone to find someone was if the people from Bulgaria managed to call before they left, but most of the villagers in southern Bulgaria did not have telephones in their homes. They also needed to have the telephone numbers of the corresponding party in Turkey, and I didn't know whether my parents had my aunt's telephone number. Even if they did, I was not sure they knew how to call or where to find a phone.

I wondered how long I could stay and wait to look for them. Even the thought that maybe I would not be able to locate them that summer crossed the dark corners of my mind, which made me frustrated. I had come from so far away I could not back down now. I would continue to search for them until I found them.

For almost a month we didn't hear any news from my aunt's sources around Istanbul. She knew most of the muhacir, immigrants, from the 1970s. They had kept a close connection after moving to Turkey.

I was on the verge of losing hope. Now I wondered if maybe I would just have to wait in the States and come here when I got the news from my aunt that my parents had arrived in Turkey. Of course, I still would be restless and anxious in the States.

My aunt found out that Leyla's relatives lived in an upscale district of Istanbul, Nişantaşı, so they must have been well off to settle there. They had moved to Turkey from Bulgaria in the1950s, during one of the earlier immigration waves. They were gradually able to build a small factory for women's ready-to-wear clothes and by the 1980s their business expanded substantially and they had many sales locations. My aunt thought that Leyla's relatives might have helped them to establish themselves in Istanbul, so she went to find out where they were located. She was able to find the location; she even found out that Leyla was employed in the family business. We just had to find out where Leyla was employed and where her parents were residing. My aunt, through a network of never-failing Turkish women's connections, was able to find out that Leyla's relatives had a retail location in the Kapalıçarşı, the Grand Bazaar, the great shopping mecca for all tourists in the heart of Istanbul's Eminönü district. She also discovered that Leyla's family was residing in the same district my aunt lived in, Bakırköy. Leyla lived nearby, probably not far from where my aunt lived, as this district was continually developing and growing.

My aunt thought if I just showed up in the store in Grand Bazaar it might shock Leyla, so my aunt decided she should go there first and find out whether Leyla was there, then let Leyla know I was here. My aunt also wanted to find out if Leyla was already married.

That Monday morning, my aunt headed for the Grand Bazaar while I stayed at their house to wait for news. It was a nerve-wracking wait. I could not concentrate to watch the television or read. I barely could sit in one place, and thoughts like What if she is not there? and What if she is there and she doesn't care to see me? were rushing through my head. Or, the most dreadful of all, What if she was already married? By thinking these thoughts, I drove myself into a frenzy. I needed to know what Leyla thought and felt about me. Did she have the same feelings she had before our separation?

After many hours, I heard the gate out front and rushed to the door to find out what my aunt discovered. Did she find my Leyla?

"Did you see her? Was she there? What did she say? Can I go see her?" tumbled from my lips as my aunt took off her coat and changed into her house slippers. I waited impatiently for her answer.

My aunt stood back and looked at me, patted my shoulder, and walked past me into the kitchen to start preparing supper. I followed her, of course, and demanded to know what happened.

"I saw Leyla," my aunt informed me. "She does work at the Grand Bazaar, but she was not alone. Leyla was leaving for lunch with some man."

"What man?" I demanded, dread filling my stomach that perhaps Leyla had moved on and forgotten me during our time apart. "What if she has someone else? What if she is married? What will I do? We need to go now! I must see Leyla, I need to know."

"Patience, Osman, everything will be fine," my aunt replied as she began washing and preparing the vegetables. "Let me work on this. Let me find out who he is before we go rushing in there and you lose her forever. Give me some time."

*   *   *

"I know that you are getting a little restless," my aunt said one morning a few days later. "But be patient. I want to take you somewhere today."

We headed for the Eminönü neighborhood in a taxi, to the Grand Bazaar where Leyla's work was situated. The longest part of our trip took us down the picturesque Kennedy Avenue connecting Bakırköy to Eminönü, and the long avenue edges the coast of Marmara Sea like a long snake. After being trapped in the narrow and busy streets of Bakırköy, our fast-moving cab flew along Kennedy Avenue. The blue of the sky and the blue of the sea merged in the distance. The view was stunning. The sea gradually narrowed here and one could see numerous large and small cargo and cruise ships intermixed with the tankers on the right, and to the left the walls of an ancient fortress and numerous businesses and old houses. After the fast ride in the taxi, we got to the Eminönü district of Istanbul, the most popular district for tourists. We left the taxi at an intersection not far from the Grand Bazaar and entered through one of the impressive gates. After walking through a still quiet bazaar lined with a variety of stores, we arrived at a store that sold women's clothing in the wholesale district behind the bazaar.

Right there, inside this store, was my beautiful Leyla. I was stunned and could not believe that it was she. She was more beautiful and breathtaking than before. She was standing behind the counter and looking straight ahead in front of her. She was not a young schoolgirl anymore; she was a young woman now. There were a few customers inside browsing through the women's clothing. At first, I thought my eyes deceived me. But there she really was, in the most unlikely place for two young people born in the small villages of southern Bulgaria to meet — in the shopping mecca of Istanbul, the Grand Bazaar.

I rushed inside and stopped right in front of Leyla. She lifted her gaze and looked at me, and complete astonishment crossed her face. I could see in her eyes that she, too, had a difficult time believing I was right there in front of her. Her face turned pale and she leaned on the counter to support herself. We looked at each other for a long time saying nothing.

Finally, she said, in a quiet voice, "Osman, is that really you?"

"Yes, Leyla," I responded with a smile.

"People said that you had been killed on the border," she said slowly.

"Those were rumors spread by the Communists, and perpetuated by people's ignorance," I said.

Until now everything looked like a black-and-white movie. There were few colors in my life, everything had looked dull and drab. I had thought this was the normal condition of the world. But, quite suddenly, I realized I was wrong. I realized Leyla's presence had this magical power to shed light and illuminate the colors in my drab world. I slowly felt in my gut that suffering and sadness was not permanent anymore for me, there was beauty and love and joy for me.

Leyla moved from behind the counter toward me and we embraced clumsily like children who didn't know what we were doing. Leyla immediately told one of the other shopkeepers that she would like to leave for a while, so we could go for a walk by ourselves.

"Go, I will be waiting for you here," my aunt said with a smile.

We walked out slowly as if in a trance. Outside, the summer sun shone with the most brilliant light and we headed toward Sultan Ahmet Square. I felt as though I had just left a dark movie theatre and ended up in this beautiful square with the great Sultan Ahmet Mosque on one side and the Hagia Sofia museum on the other. We decided to sit on the benches by the beautiful fountain, surrounded by grass and beautiful, fragrant flowers between these two iconic buildings.

"I am so happy to see you," I said slowly, afraid that I was going to frighten her off like a bird that would fly away or that she was a beautiful dream and I would suddenly awaken. "I missed you so much. I thought of you every single day and you were in my dreams every night. I dreamed of you smiling and walking in the tobacco fields and green meadows of the mountain, by that waterfall and on the shore of Arda River. You were ephemera, a fleeting moment, magical, and, at the same time, elusive. We were together until I was awakened from my dreams. It was so difficult to wake up and realize that we were a world apart."

She looked at me then slowly turned and looked at the ground.

"I missed you and I thought about you all the time, too," she said. "I felt lonely and abandoned when you left."

"I am really sorry you had to go through all that. But it was not easy for me, either. I had to survive, I had to protect you; I didn't have any other choice." We were silent for a few minutes, both needing time for the words to sink in and form meaning in our heads. I was fighting the tears coming to my eyes.

"Please tell me about your life first," I said, breaking the silence that was getting too heavy. "What happened to you after we separated in my village, when Mustafa and I headed for the border?"

165

"After I spent two days with Hasan's family," she began, "I went back to my parents' house where I stayed until the exodus of Turks this June. I worked in the tobacco fields with my parents in the summers and in the winters we processed the dry tobacco. I felt so lonely after you left, and then there were rumors that you had been killed. Somehow, I refused to believe them in the beginning, but the cloud of doubt grew with time and I thought maybe you had perished." She fell silent, staring in front of her.

"How was life after the name change?" I asked with curiosity.

"First, as you know, the names of all Turks living in Bulgaria were changed," she said. "The campaign was completed in the winter of 1985; many were killed and wounded in the process and thousands ended up in the Belene concentration camp or prisons. The Communists prohibited the speaking of Turkish everywhere and imposed fines on all people who spoke it in public places. Repeat offenders got heavy fines and many were sent to prison for defying orders.

"What happened to all our books in the Turkish language?" I asked, remembering newspaper articles about the burning of Turkish books I had loved reading.

"The Communists continued to burn all books in Turkish they were able to find during surprise raids on the houses of the Turks," she continued sadly. "After they burned all the books they could find, they turned to the Turkish gravestones and chiseled off all the names written in modern Turkish or Ottoman Turkish. The names of our ancestors were changed to Bulgarian in all the archives. The Communists even started to build a big building in Krumovgrad to gather all the Turkish children and teach them only the Bulgarian language."

There were crowds of tourists walking slowly and enjoying the great beauty of the square, and local people walking briskly about their business, while Leyla shared the horrific events she had lived through since I last saw her. My heart broke for her and all that she had been through. Why had I left her to such a fate? I should have found a way to take her with me.

Right then and there, I decided to ask the question that had been burning inside of me for years. I looked in Leyla's lovely eyes, held her delicate hand in mine, and I gently asked her, "Will you marry me, Leyla? "

She looked at me with disbelieving eyes. I could see the anguish she held inside. Finally, she sighed and turned her eyes back toward the ground.

"First, there is something I need to tell you about myself before I respond to your question." She looked up at me with tenderness and I saw that tears were welling in her eyes.

"Since we Turks like rumors, I want you to know from me, not from any rumors on the streets. My parents are arranging a marriage for me to the son of a rich businessman from Istanbul. His name is Mesut and I have been seeing him for some time."

It took a moment for Leyla's words to sink in and create meaning. I didn't want for them to be true. I thought that I misunderstood her. I wanted the words to be wrong, to be different. After finally finding each other after so many years apart, how could she be promised to another?

"I am so sorry, I am so sorry that you went through all this," I said, "but I love you so much and want you even more than ever to be my wife." I looked at Leyla, at her beautiful glowing bright eyes. "I love you and I want for us to be together. I have been thinking of you day and night for five long years. What do you intend to do?" I could not hide the pain and fear that I could lose Leyla again.

"I don't want to hurt my parents — they went through hell in Bulgaria. They want me to have a better life than they had back there working in the tobacco fields."

"I am not rich," I said with a sober voice, "but I promise to love you. I cannot imagine life without you. I will make you happy."

"Yes, but I cannot think only about myself. I have to think about my parents; they have gone through hell so I can be free and happy," she said, with her conflicting emotions evident on her face.

"But how you can be happy if you are going to marry somebody you don't love?" I asked, incredulous.

"I have to make sacrifices," she said. "Everyone makes sacrifices sooner or later, Osman. Our lives are not always our own. How can I betray my parents, and Mesut is a good man, he cares for me. How is it fair to him for me just to suddenly break things off with him."

"You don't have to sacrifice your happiness," I said, becoming irritated with her stubbornness. "I don't see how you sacrificing your happiness can make your parents happy. If they really want your happiness, they should ask you what you want for yourself. Do you really want to marry someone whom you don't love?"

"Osman, people in this country get into arranged marriages all the time, and they are happy." She sighed.

"Leyla, you are not everybody," I replied adamantly. "You are an intelligent woman, you know what you want, and you should have a say in

168

whether you want to marry Mesut or not."

I knew Leyla was smart. The fact that she was so considerate of her parents made me love her even more. I knew she loved me, but she was torn, not because she was afraid of her parents, but because she respected them and she didn't want to hurt them. They really had gone through hell to get their daughter here, to provide her a better life and see her safe. They were arranging the marriage for Leyla because they thought it would be the right thing to do. Leyla wanted to obey her parents, but she was torn inside. I sensed it. In the midst of all of this, my heart was breaking into a million little pieces. I knew that deep in her heart Leyla didn't want this marriage. She didn't want to admit to herself that she didn't want it, but seeing me, she was even more confused. All this was so sudden, and I needed to give Leyla more time.

*   *   *

I gradually was getting used to the frantic pace of life in this city, to the perpetual impatience of the drivers, to the heat of the summer which contributed to the hotheadedness of the local Turks.

When we met again the next day and sat at the same bench, I pressed the issue of her arranged marriage, asking her, "Isn't an arranged marriage backwardness and a sign of less developed society and civilization?"

"No, not really," said Leyla, looking at me as though I was accusing her of being backward and didn't know what I was talking about. "Comparing two civilizations, I assume you mean Western and Eastern or Islamic, is like comparing apples to oranges, as the old cliché goes. Suggesting one civilization is better is simply the wrong way of thinking. They are just different, and if things are done differently, it doesn't mean that one is superior to another."

I didn't want Leyla's statement to make sense, even though I knew it did. I knew Leyla had feelings for me, and I didn't know whether she would go ahead with the arranged marriage. I knew she was conflicted — if she wanted Mesut and an arranged marriage, then why would she agree to meet me here again?

For weeks, we continued to meet at the same bench between Sultan Ahmet Mosque and the museum Hagia Sofia, whenever the bench was free of the swarms of tourists. Sometimes I would take her to the local pastry shops where we would have baklava and a soft drink and continue our discussions there.

Gradually I persuaded Leyla that she would not be happy in a loveless, arranged marriage, even though her parents thought it was appropriate for her. She began to realize that turning down the arranged marriage with Mesut did not mean she no longer loved or respected her parents, even though they would object to her decision.

I watched as Leyla became more animated each time we met, her face beginning to glow with anticipation. I had managed to convince her that my marriage proposal was sincere and would offer her true happiness.

During one of our later meetings, I told Leyla that she needed a passport and an American fiancée visa to travel to the States, if she wanted to be with me. She looked at me with hope and fear.

"My family has Turkish citizenship now," she said. "I should be able to get a Turkish passport now, but I have to get the passport and visa secretly, so my parents don't find out. When they find out that I escaped with you, they will be heartbroken, but if I stay here and marry Mesut I could be heartbroken for the rest of my life."

I felt great joy inside because I was going to be with Leyla. "Why don't I have my aunt go to your parents and request your hand in marriage?" I said with a glimmer of hope, knowing this was an acceptable custom in Turkish tradition.

"My parents will not agree," she said. "They have made up their minds, and they want me to marry Mesut because his parents are rich and conservative." She looked up at me, waiting.

"Then we have to leave without telling your parents," I announced. "Do you think you can live with that?"

"Yes," she replied. "For a while I thought I loved Mesut, but now I realize it was infatuation. I would have quickly gotten tired of living with him and been miserable the rest of my life — burning in the hell of a marriage without love."

Finally, Leyla had changed her mind and agreed to go with me to America. Within a few short days, she was able to gather all papers and get her passport. Then we applied for a fiancée visa from the American consulate in Istanbul. It took a few weeks, but the visa was issued.

It was the happiest day of my stay in Turkey.

Chapter 21

When I wasn't meeting with Leyla, I was searching the refugee camp near Edirne run by the Turkish Red Crescent, trying to locate my parents. One day, I was asking newcomers where they came from, and whether they knew anything about the people from my village. Suddenly, I saw a person I recognized, Şükrü, a teenager from my village. At first I thought I might have made a mistake, but I looked more carefully and knew it was unmistakably Şükrü. He appeared tired and beat down.

"Şükrü!" I said, elated that finally I saw somebody I knew. "How are you doing? When did you arrive in Turkey?"

He looked at me for the longest time, as if he was seeing a ghost, somebody who was not supposed to be there.

"I am doing okay, I guess," he finally said with a weary voice. "I made it to Turkey this week, with my family. Osman, what are you doing here? We thought you were dead. There were rumors you had been killed at the border on your way to Greece."

"No, I am fine," I said, and then somberly added, "but unfortunately Mustafa didn't make it." I sighed and hesitated for a moment.

"I made it to America and now live in Chicago," I added. Şükrü looked at me with disbelieving eyes.

"America," he said slowly with veneration, looking at me from head to toe. He looked at my T-shirt, blue jeans, and tennis shoes as if he was seeing somebody from the movies. I guessed he had a tough time believing everything.

"Şükrü, have you seen my parents? Are they coming here?" I asked impatiently, wanting any news he had to share. But he just continued to stare at me.

"They are fine," he replied eventually. "They were getting ready to move here, too, when I left. Your father had to wait in a long line for his passport. Then they had to wait for transportation, because all the trucks were busy waiting at the border. They had to wait on the Bulgarian side of the border because of the long line, about 30 kilometers in length."

He looked at me as if he was witnessing a miracle. "We believed that you were dead for the longest time," he said. "The officials didn't let us know that you made it out alive to the other side."

"I made it, Şükrü, I made it. I am very much alive and so happy to see you."

Then Şükrü told me about the deplorable situation of the Turks waiting in line at the Bulgarian side of the border. He said that people didn't have basic necessities, like food and water or toilets. They had to walk for many kilometers to get drinking water. Forget about a shower. Şükrü's family ate the food they had brought with them from home, and he was grateful they had made it to the border just before it ran out. He said he was one of the lucky ones because he had been able to bring lots of meat and other food preserved in jars. Many of the Turks coming from the towns didn't carry any food and were practically starving.

He was shocked to see so many people in the tent cities on the Turkish side.

We both realized that it was getting more and more difficult for the Turkish government to deal with the endless influx of this huge mass of Turks from Bulgaria. Turkey couldn't handle many more refugees.

Chapter 22

Slowly, Istanbul was beginning to feel like a second home to me. Even though most of the salespeople and all the Turks with whom I was in contact were able to detect the different dialect of my Turkish, they accepted me as one of them. In essence, I was not yabancı, a foreigner, even though technically I was yabancı. All this made my visit bearable in the beginning and the more time I spent there, the more pleasant the stay became. I had fun with the salespeople in the stores and with the street vendors and waiters, asking them to guess where I came from. Some of them thought I was from Cyprus or Yugoslavia, but most knew that I had the accent of a Turk from Bulgaria. They knew about the influx of refugees from Bulgaria and were worried, not without reason, about the local economy, about their jobs and businesses being affected by this unprecedented, sudden, and unexpected addition of hundreds of thousands of people into their country.

One shopkeeper, when he found out that I was from Bulgaria, said, "Why are you coming here? We don't have enough jobs for our people. Where will we get jobs for you, the newcomers? You are not welcome here. Why don't you go back to Bulgaria? You are not Turks you, are

Bulgarians. You have no business moving to Turkey." I got angry.

"You obviously don't understand the pain these people have suffered before they decided to move here," I responded. "You don't know anything about being oppressed, having everything taken from you and being treated like an animal and worse in the country where you were born. You should be ashamed of yourself for saying these things." Then without waiting for a response, I quickly left. I didn't want to get involved in an endless dispute that no one would win. It was obvious that many people in Turkey were not happy that Turks from Bulgaria were moving there.

Istanbul was like rakı, a Turkish alcoholic drink — it could be harsh, bitter and shocking in the beginning, but once you got past the bitter beginning, it got better and you felt better, and after a few days you got addicted to the city. You want more of the city and you can never get enough. Eventually, you fall in love with the city and when you are far away from it, you dream of it. You miss the frantic pace, the taste of kebabs and baklava, the smell of the city, the gentle breath of the Bosphorus, the endless rows of beautiful houses, and palaces on the strait. The city could be like a beautiful dream, if you didn't have to worry about your parents, your sweetheart or your own future, although to a certain extend the city has the magical power to make you forget about your worries. It has the capacity to soothe you, to relax you and make you enjoy it, and slowly it assimilates you.

The days I did not go to Edirne or meet with Leyla, I would go for long walks in the city. I walked from the Grand Bazaar down to the spice market and from there it was a short walk to the beautiful Yeni Cami, New

Mosque, with hundreds of pigeons being fed by the children and tourists. I walked the long underground walkway and got to the Sirkeci docks, crossing Kennedy Avenue through an underground crossing with numerous stores in it, where the ferryboats coming from the Asian side stop. There was always a huge crowd of people coming and going. This city was vibrant, throbbing with life, youthful, feminine, and hip.

I loved the smell of the sea on the magnificent Bosphorus; I would walk across Galata bridge and take deep breaths, inhaling the lovely smell of the sea deep into my lungs. Pausing over the waters of the Golden Horn, I enjoyed enormously the gentle caress of the sea breeze and late summer sun on my skin and hair. In the middle of the bridge, I would stop and turn toward the awe-inspiring, majestic Bosphorus. For a moment I thought that all of what was happening to me was a wild dream.

I couldn't stop thinking about Leyla. Happiness was within reach, I thought, even though I didn't quite have it yet. I was in love. I was crazy in love. I felt that all those silly Turkish love songs were written for us. I saw Leyla and myself in the middle of every love song. How was it possible that every single stroke of the baglama, our Turkish musical instrument, described my love? Every single beat of darbuka, the drum, was like the beat of my heart. I felt like laughing and crying at the same time. For a moment the thought that I had gone mad passed through my head. Had I gone mad? Yes, but I needed to look sane, I thought. I had come too far to give up now.

I entertained thoughts of moving to Istanbul and living here happily ever after with Leyla. I walked the steep and narrow roads to Istiklal Caddesi, Independence Avenue, in the Beyoğlu district, where numerous churches, mosques, and synagogues peacefully coexisted. I loved Istiklal Caddesi, with its classical 19th-century European-style architecture and its countless pastries, kebab restaurants, gift shops, and fashion boutiques, reminiscent of the boutiques on the magnificent mile of Chicago. Seeing many young couples walking hand in hand or embracing made me think of Leyla. I could be walking with Leyla, like those couples, and settle here. I was happy that I found Leyla, and I wanted us to be together all the time.

I would walk all the way to Taksim Square, wide and round, in the middle of which was a big monument to the liberators of Turkey: a large, full-body-length sculpture of the founders of modern Turkey, including Mustafa Kemal Atatürk in the front. Gezi Park, which I thought was wonderful, offered a small, green island of trees, grass and flowers, an oasis amongst an ocean of concrete.

The longer I waited, the greater the chance of Leyla's parents discovering our plans.

Chapter 23

In August there were lengthy articles in the Turkish newspapers about the influx of Turks from Bulgaria and its economic strain on Turkish economy. In the Turkish media there were estimates and predictions that more than 1,000,000 Turks would be there by the end of 1989. There were rumors that the Turkish government would be closing the border soon. Suddenly the Turkish government decided they needed to stop the influx of people or they would have a huge economic mess, maybe even a humanitarian catastrophe, on their hands. The Turkish authorities said that they needed to decrease the number of refugees from Bulgaria.

On August 21, 1989, Turkish authorities, in a state of emergency, decided to close the border, even though thousands of people were still waiting to cross it. From June 3 to August 21, 1989, about 360,000 "tourists" emigrated from Bulgaria to Turkey without needing a visa.

I went to Edirne refugee camp for the last time, hoping that my parents had made it, but they were not there. This meant they had not made it before the border closed. The Turkish government said the border was not really closed, that all Bulgarian citizens who wished to visit Turkey could obtain a visa from the Turkish consulates in Bulgaria. The Turkish government managed to reduce the flood to a trickle by imposing this entry visa. I realized that my parents were not coming to Turkey any time soon. That meant that if I wanted to see them, I had to travel to Bulgaria. I was reluctant to go back, but it was the only way to see my parents.

I found the Bulgarian consulate in Istanbul, in Etiler district, a long drive from my aunt's house in Bakırköy. I had to change shared taxis a couple of times before I got there. The looks of the Bulgarian consulate didn't fill me with admiration or delight. It was a relatively small, gray, unattractive building. I guessed it was built in the latest fashion of the socialist architectural progress and advance. It looked like a bomb shelter. The building was fenced in with a high, ugly brick wall — a continuation of the Iron Curtain, I thought. My anxiety rose a notch when I saw the ugly building and the small Bulgarian flag flying on a pole in the yard. But I needed to see my parents.

I approached a small room with an awning and a small window, which was cracked open enough to hand over passports. Paranoia from the outside world was still in full swing here in the Bulgarian consulate. I was grateful that there were a few other intrepid souls waiting in the small line, so I was not alone under the watchful eyes of Turkish police officers who looked straight at me suspiciously. Before I got to the small opening, I had to go through a checkpoint manned by two officers who asked me the purpose of my visit. I told them I wanted to get a tourist visa to Bulgaria. After careful inspection of my American passport, the officers let me in through narrow doors that led to a small courtyard with a single room built into the wall surrounding the consulate.

When it was my turn to tell them why I was there, a lady in her fifties with big eyeglasses and curly hair asked me in a stern voice and strongly Bulgarian-accented English, where I intended to go in Bulgaria. I told her, with my newly acquired American English, that I wanted a tourist visa to see Sofia and spend a week in the great Bulgarian sea resort on the Black Sea, Sunny Beach. Then I was given a paper called a declaration on which I had to answer many questions, like where I wanted to go, where I intended to stay, how much money I had, and that if I didn't declare the right amount of money, it would be confiscated by the customs officers. I had to keep the receipts with stamps from the hotels where I stayed. Otherwise, I would get a big fine or, even worse, I could be apprehended by the customs officials.

At this point I was intimidated, but not enough to change my mind. I was relying on my new American passport to keep me out of trouble. I was counting on the fact that Bulgaria was not on the U.S. list of favorite countries, and Bulgaria didn't want to further antagonize U.S. officials by arresting its citizens on Bulgarian soil. I gave my passport over, filled out the declaration and gave it to the grouchy lady, who looked stressed out. I was just praying that I would get the visa. When I came back that afternoon, I received the visa that gave me permission to visit Bulgaria for 15 days. I was elated and scared witless. Next, I needed to decide how I was going to get to Bulgaria.

One of the least conspicuous ways to travel was by train. It was easy to blend into the big international crowd. I decided to travel from the Istanbul Sirkeci train station to Sofia. There were many international trains going through Sofia and I decided to travel by Balkan Express because it stopped in Plovdiv, where I could slip off the train and catch a bus to Krumovgrad.

The Balkan Express was a much more modest variation, as I would find out later, of the luxurious Orient Express which used to travel to the very same station from which I was leaving Istanbul. Sirkeci was the last stop of the historical, world-renowned Orient Express known for luxury and intrigue from the book *Murder on the Orient Express* by the great British writer Agatha Christie. At the end of the journey on the famous train, one arrived in one of the most exotic cities in Europe, Istanbul.

I liked the busy and ornate exterior of Sirkeci train terminal. It was a great representation of Ottoman architecture from the final decades of the empire. I was pleasantly surprised by the space inside the station's terminal building. Like many other buildings, mosques, and churches in this city, it felt larger inside than it seemed from the outside.

Finally, my day of departure arrived and I boarded the Balkan Express. The train left the station on time that morning. It was a warm, sunny September day in 1989, a year when Eastern Europe and the world were quickly changing. It felt as if everything was happening suddenly, almost overnight, but the people of Eastern Europe had been waiting and preparing for this change for decades.

The train sped through Istanbul's endless sea of houses, buildings, and businesses. It took more than an hour to get to the edge of the city as we sped through the Thrace region of Turkey, toward the Bulgarian frontier. Turkish Thrace was covered with huge fields of sunflowers — yellow, as far as the eye could see, from the left to right. We arrived at the Turkish border before noon and got our exit stamps from the Turks before heading for the Bulgarian border check. It took mere minutes to get there. My anxiety was at a fever pitch, my hands started to sweat. I didn't know what to expect and I was scared witless. What would happen to me — would they find out I escaped from this country five years ago? Would I be arrested and thrown in prison? I tried to look calm and relaxed as much as possible, but it was not easy. Sweat was trickling down my back and my breathing got short. I had a difficult time getting enough air.

After we'd passed to the Bulgarian side, it felt as if somebody had decreased the intensity of light a couple of notches and everything looked gray and drab, almost like in the bleak black-and-white movies from Stalinist times. Two towering customs officers opened the door of the compartment and stared sternly at the people in the compartment. My passport and declaration, given to me earlier by the conductor, was in my sweaty hand. One officer had long, thick hair that protruded from under his hat, a three-day-old beard, and a huge black mustache. He looked intimidating. He took my documents and went somewhere with my papers. The other officer looked toward my backpack, which was stored on the baggage rack above my head, and barked "Baggage!" and made a gesture like he was opening a bag. I took my backpack and opened it. I hoped that my clothing would not make much of an impression on the customs officers, because I had bought my clothing in Turkey from Turks leaving Bulgaria so I could blend in when I got in Bulgaria. He went through everything one by one, my underwear, socks, the small camera, and a few rolls of film. Since I was a tourist, I thought that camera and films would be expected. He went through my toiletries, opened the toothpaste, and looked very carefully at my shaving cream. I didn't think he liked it. Then the bigger and scarier officer returned and gave my papers back to me, and they left the compartment.

My stuff was thrown all over the seat. With hands shaking, I put my clothing and toiletries back in my bag. I guess we are done, I thought, though we still had to wait for the whole train to be checked. We waited maybe for half an hour to 45 minutes, which felt like an eternity to me. Gentle relief washed over me as the train slowly moved, accelerated and left behind the drab, uniform, and mostly ugly buildings on the Bulgarian side of the Bulgarian–Turkish border.

The train rushed through Bulgarian Thrace. At that point, I didn't hate anyone, even the initiator of the horrendous name change campaign. I felt sorry for them; they must have gone through personal hell to decide to commit a crime like that.

Bulgarian Thrace was beautiful, too. It was mostly even terrain. There were many fields with uncollected vegetables, mostly peppers, big, green and red, the kind of peppers that grew only in Bulgaria, much larger than the ones in my new home. Considering it was fall, farmers were late in harvesting these vegetables.

By late afternoon, we were quickly approaching Plovdiv. It was the first stop of the train in Bulgaria, where I had decided to slip out into the crowd at the station. I had changed into my "Bulgarian" clothing in the train toilet, and I had converted some U.S. dollars to Bulgarian leva in Istanbul, from Turks of Bulgaria. The train stopped slowly at the station. At first I was stricken at how bad the whole town looked, dilapidated and run down. I didn't know if this place had changed, or if I was just used to living in well-built surroundings in the States. The platform was uneven, covered with dark gray blocks of cement, some broken, some missing altogether. It didn't bother the people at all, they were used to it. They just walked, oblivious, tired and grim, like zombies in a nightmare. I was shocked, but I tried hard not to let it show, just lowered my gaze and walked like another zombie myself. I was thankful to be on the move again. I had calmed down during the monotonous movement of the train through the big fields of Bulgarian Thrace region after the excitement of passing the border. I exited the train toward the busy central part of Plovdiv station and tried to blend in with the crowd of sullen travelers who were heading toward the exit. This place was not completely unfamiliar to me. I had been here once with friends from high school. We had traveled to Plovdiv by train to see the Plovdiv fair of international commercial companies. The exhibition of Western companies and technologies had been a little glimpse of the West during the strong years of Communism in Bulgaria.

I headed toward the door of the station and exited. There were a few taxi cabs, old beat up Ladas and Moskviches, Soviet-made cars. One was ugly, the other one uglier. I told one of the drivers that I needed to go to Rhodope bus station. I knew the name of the bus station from my school trip to the city. The bus station didn't look any better than the train station, dilapidated, old and run down. The ticket office window was a tiny opening where I could buy my ticket.

"I would like one ticket to Krumovgrad, please," I said with my best Bulgarian and handed over twenty Bulgarian leva. The cashier, in her late forties glanced at me with a serious expression, and handed me the precious ticket and change. My excitement grew again — I was about to visit my birthplace, where I had spent my childhood in the Eastern Rhodope Mountains. The small bus stop where the bus would pull off the road and let me off was situated a few kilometers from Çaliköy, and I

185

could walk from the bus stop to my village, the place I once called home. I suddenly missed the smell of dry tobacco and linden and almond trees during their spring bloom. I missed the green meadows around the village where my friends and I once played çelik and soccer. At the same time, I was nervous about how I would be received there, and what the local authorities would do about my visit.

The voyage from Plovdiv to my village felt like an eternity. The old Chavdar Bulgarian-made bus passed through Haskovo and then crept along the winding narrow road through the eastern Rhodope Mountains. I looked at the tobacco fields and most of the tobacco was not harvested. The tobacco plants looked sad in expectation of the caring owner coming and collecting the leaves. The bus went by hamlet after hamlet; I looked outside and could not see any people. They had vanished. The houses looked deserted and many windows and doors were missing. The windows of the houses looked like hollow openings of a human skull, accusing and frightening. With the people gone, it seemed that the whole life was gone. Gone were the little children playing on the dusty roads and all the animals. Not even wild animals could be seen. Hamlet after hamlet, this view was repeated. It was eerie and heart-wrenching to witness.

When the bus approached the Çaliköy stop, I signaled to the driver that I wanted to get off. He looked at me in disbelief and asked, "Are you sure that you want to get off here?"

"Yes, I am."

The bus came to a screeching halt at the bus stop, causing a small dust cloud and smog storm. I took my backpack and exited the bus, which quickly sped off leaving me behind. It was still a pleasantly warm

September afternoon.

The old water fountain was not running, the tube for the water was clogged with duckweed. Even the water fountain looked abandoned and in need of attention. The narrow, winding asphalt road was full of potholes and also needed repair. I walked through the dusty narrow path toward my village. No human could be seen anywhere. The place was the most desolate place on the earth. The path wound around the small hills, which were full of thorn bushes slowly reclaiming the landscape. I got close to the narrow hanging bridge and saw that some of the wooden planks were missing. Then I decided walking through the river was a safer bet than walking on the bridge with the gaping holes. There was little water left after the long summer had dried up the river. The water was clear and I could see the sandy bottom. There were wide sandy banks, and I took off my shoes the way I used to do when I was younger and walked through the hot sand. I walked slowly, enjoying the warmth and softness of the fine sand under my feet. I jumped in the water; it was warm and pleasant.

I used to swim in the small pools of water from this river every summer, countless times over the years, often with Mustafa. I had immensely enjoyed the hot sun and my skin would acquire a deep tan. The river looked the same as I remembered it from my childhood, but it was sadder and abandoned. Being here was a surreal experience; it was difficult to believe that I was back in the country of my childhood. It was like a dream where you were in a place that you knew, but the place was somewhat different and alien and you had a difficult time defining what was different from before.

I expected to be rudely awakened from this dream at any moment and see things as they used to be, as they should have been. I walked slowly through the river and reached the water's edge where, on warm round stones, I put my shoes on and walked through the narrow path toward my village.

Thoughts were running through my head. Once there were many people here, but now they were gone. Why were they now gone? What was the purpose of having empty houses and land overgrown with weeds? This was nobody's land now, with no owners. They had left for good and were not coming back. The land was crying, left alone with no one to take care of it.

I decided to take a detour and visit the hamlet between the river and my village. The hamlet was situated on a plateau, around which small plantations of tobacco were mostly intact. Some of the tobacco had failed to develop. It looked pathetic, sickly. When I reached the plateau, I looked back to the river. The river looked like a long snake which had shed its skin, with the bank the empty skin. The hamlet looked completely unoccupied, as I walked slowly through it. Once there had been the happy chatter of women, men and children, who would yell to the cattle, and there would be music coming from old Russian- and Bulgarian-made radios. The air would smell like home-cooked stew, pancakes, bread. Now the hamlet was desolate and dead, and there was no particular smell I could detect.

I walked into one of the houses. It was completely bare, even the sockets for electrical power were vacant. The open windows moved slowly in the breeze, the glass half broken, an invisible ghost moving them. The roof was sagging, the house looked sad and depressed because the owners had left it. It amazed me how quickly houses deteriorated once the owners left. I approached one of the windows and looked through it. There was a nice view of the river winding by; I thought that the owners probably missed this view very much. Then I sensed that I was not alone in the house and quickly turned around in surprise to see a small boy, maybe ten years old. I thought I was seeing a ghost, that the house was haunted. I was startled and quickly said, "Hello. You scared me."

I looked carefully at the boy, who was standing there silently.

"What is your name?" I asked quietly. Finally the boy tried to talk, but whatever he was saying didn't make any sense.

"Where do you live? Where are your parents?" I asked, at the same time trying to calm myself from the sudden surprise. I finally had met somebody here, but did he have a speech impediment? Then the boy made a gesture of "follow me" and took off. I followed him as he walked briskly to the end of the hamlet where a short thin man sat in front of the house on an old wooden bench. He was maybe fifty or sixty, and his aged face was wrinkled. When he saw me, he stood up.

"Selamun aleykum aga," I said as I approached.

"Aleykum selam," he said in a raspy voice. "Welcome, welcome." He looked me over from head to toe. "You are not from around here."

"No, I am not," I said. "But five years ago I used to live in Çaliköy. My name is Osman, and I am Kazim's son."

"Aah, I remember, you are the one who escaped to Greece. But there were rumors that you had been killed on the border. I am very glad to see that you made it through. I remember I saw your mother crying loud on the road outside your house. The cry of that poor woman pierced my heart.

No parent deserves to suffer like that."

I became a little uncomfortable from discussing my family with this strange man.

"How come you are the only people left in the hamlet? Why didn't you go to Turkey with the rest of the people?" I asked.

Then he lowered his gaze and slowly walked back to his bench, and I noticed that he was limping.

"My brother used to live in one of these houses. He begged me to leave for Turkey, but I refused. Look at us, one of us barely can walk and the other one cannot talk. Where we will go? I don't want to be a burden to my brother and his family. He has plenty of other people to take care of."

I felt sorry for the man and a little guilty that I had been so brusque with him.

"I never have lived outside of my village," he said. "The only work I know is tobacco and we have plenty of animals to supply us with milk and cheese. We have a small garden to grow vegetables and for Bayram we will go to Çaliköy or Ada where there are people. My wife died when she was giving birth and my only son is mute, as you maybe noticed."

"You must be feeling lonely. Don't you miss the people who used to live here?"

"There isn't a day when I don't think about them, but there is nothing I can do. The empty houses and the howl of the dogs that were abandoned, their cry for their owners in the night, breaks my heart. But what I can do, this is our destiny."

I was saddened by the words of this stranger, but I decided that it was time for me to go up the mountain to my village.

"Good bye, aga, and take good care of yourselves," I said to the poor man and his son.

Chapter 24

I walked fast now toward Çalıköy. My apprehension and anxiety grew the closer I got to the village. I took the narrow sheep and goat path surrounded with thorn, dogwood and wild berry bushes, stopping in a couple of places to taste raspberries that tasted exactly as I remembered. The narrow, winding uphill path passed by the old cemetery. I remembered Leyla saying that all the names on the gravestones in the Turkish cemetery had been chiseled off. Out of curiosity, I decided that I would have a look. I walked slowly, with a little apprehension to see what damage I might find. As a child, I always had been scared to walk by the cemetery because some of the older kids would say that there was a peri, a fairy, and ghosts which would show up at night to abduct small children and take them under the ground where the dead bodies were. I walked slowly and looked at the gravestones and saw that the old Turkish engraved names, some from as far back as the Ottoman Empire, had been chiseled out. So it was true, I thought, slightly shocked from the reality. I had hoped it wasn't true. I was even more shocked to find a couple of gravestones with Bulgarian names, as no ethnic Bulgarians had ever lived in my village.

I continued to walk toward the village, even faster now that I knew that my parents thought that I was dead.

Finally, I saw one of the houses, then two, and eventually the whole village was before me. It was an unbelievable view. The village was standing where I had left it five years ago. The village I thought I would never see again in my life. The village where I grew up, played çelik, soccer, and hide-and-seek. A place where I had been happy. I saw my parents' house, our home, exactly as I remembered it from my years here.

I quickly approached the house and saw my father there, splitting wood in front, as he had done many times over the years, to prepare for winter. As I approached, he noticed me, but I don't think he was able to recognize me at first. He looked carefully at me, then he dropped the ax and rushed toward the door of the house and quickly entered. Moments later my father reappeared with my mother behind him. They were moving slowly toward me, disbelief in their eyes as if they were seeing a ghost. When I reached them, I said, "Selamun aleykum, mother, father." They looked like the characters from the old movies without sound, where the actors looked at the camera in the most dramatic way to express their astonishment and wonder. My parents' eyes widened and then, my mother started crying.

"Osman, Osman you have returned," she repeated hysterically.

My father didn't know what to do or say. I hugged my poor mother and held her in my arms as I had done as a child. My father hugged me clumsily like a bear and looked me over, disbelieving, and then tears start welling in his eyes and my name rolled out of his mouth like a boulder, heavy and slow.

"Osman," he said, and shook me as though he wanted to make sure that I was real. "Osman, you have returned." He tried to smile, even laugh, but at the same time he was crying. When I saw my father crying, I started crying, too. We sat there on the ground for the longest time, unable to talk, just crying and hugging each other. After a while, my father decided to go and let Hasan know that I had returned. He walked quickly, almost running, to Hasan's house. My mother and I went toward the house and just decided to sit on the bench under the shade of an old almond tree. She looked older than her age; there were deep shadows under her sad eyes. After a while my father returned and finally we started talking. Then the villagers started trickling down into our yard. First a few, then more and more of them came with disbelieving eyes. All the villagers, or whoever was left in the village, wanted to shake my hand, to hug me and kiss me on the cheeks. In the beginning they were in shock and looked at me as if they were witnessing a miracle, someone who had died long ago and had come back from the dead.

"A few days after you escaped we were told by two militia that you had been killed on the border and your body was buried where you were shot," my father said.

"I could not believe they put you through this," I replied, "but such a thing should be expected from a vicious Communist regime. They killed so many innocent people, why would they hesitate to lie about me being killed, too?" There was whisper and talk of approval from the people who gathered there. The mood of the villagers gradually lifted and they all were very excited and everybody wanted to talk at the same time. There was a euphoric, almost festive atmosphere in the air. In their eyes I had truly come back from the dead. When I told them that I was living in America now, they had a difficult time believing it to be real. They were amazed that somebody from their village could go and adjust to living in the West. America, in their minds, was that faraway, unattainable place with a strange language. A country of plenty, freedom, and a fascinating concept, *democracy*.

"America, America," some of the villagers said with reverence in their voices. Everybody in the crowd knew of the two American presidents who had done so much for the freedom of the Eastern European people, Ronald Reagan and George H.W. Bush.

"It seems to me that American food has been good for you, Osman" one villager said, "since you have grown so much since you escaped and you look so well." Somebody in the crowd suggested that maybe I was tired from the journey and that I should be left alone with my family, but the majority of the villagers didn't want to hear that.

"We don't get visitors from America every day," somebody said. "We want to ask him questions about America."

The villagers in Çaliköy were simple people. One of the most educated people was my father, who had an eighth-grade education, considered a good level of education for our village. Most of the old people didn't have any formal secular education either, they had only religious schooling. The older people could speak very little Bulgarian or they could not speak any at all because they lived in a predominantly Turkish area.

One middle-aged man stood and asked, "Why did the Turkish government close the border on us?"

"The Turkish government will not be able to take all of you," I said, "not because they don't want to, but because their economy is not big enough to absorb you all at once and provide jobs or sustenance for all of you. From now on you should improve your conditions for yourselves here in Bulgaria. You will get your freedom and rights here in Bulgaria, through democratic process. Believe me, these are the last days of a dying and oppressive Communist regime, and there is no going back."

"Is it true that the American Congress voted a resolution this year, condemning the brutal treatment of the Turkish Minority in Bulgaria?" someone else asked.

Thank you, Radio Free Europe, I thought, and said, "I am astonished that you know this. Yes, it is true."

"Is it true that the American President George Bush recalled the American ambassador to Bulgaria in protest against the violation of the human rights of the Turks in Bulgaria?"

"Yes, it is true. You know so much that I would not be surprised if you know something I don't know," I said with a smile.

"Long live George Bush, our friend and enemy of Communism," somebody said.

"America is a great country!" said another and "Yes, yes!" was the answer from the majority of the people.

"America has the most advanced fighter Jet in the world, the F-16," said a young man in the crowd.

"What does the Bulgarian military have, a few rusty MIGs," someone responded and everybody laughed in unison. Their desire to know about America was insatiable. In their mind, everything America did was right and everything the Communists in their own country did was wrong. Then the villagers asked me about skyscrapers in America.

"Are they really as big as they are shown on television and in the movies?"

"Yes, they are big," I said with a smile. "Actually, they are bigger when you see them from up close. When the weather is cloudy the tips of many buildings in Chicago are lost in the clouds."

People responded with, "Breh breh" and "tschi tschi" sounds with their tongues, expressing their wonder and astonishment or disbelief.

"In the suburbs of the big cities, many houses are two stories and almost all of them grow green grass which is cut short," I said, trying to describe the way I saw America. Another wave of "breh breh" and "tschi tschi" came from the growing crowd. I quickly changed back into my American clothing in the house because I was more comfortable in it. My clothing was scrutinized by the youth of the village. They said that my blue jeans, sneakers, T-shirt, watch and backpack were very nice and didn't look like the fake cheap stuff sold in the local market. One of the younger men told me that they all would love to be dressed like me, but this stuff was not available in the local stores.

That night we stayed outside visiting until late. My father started a fire in the middle of the yard and people sat around it on whatever they could find. The people gathered around the fire were eager to hear about the world outside the boundaries of their country. Even though the older generations were not educated in secular schools, because of the *free* education given to them by Radio Free Europe, Voice of America, and BBC London, they knew exactly who supported them in their quest for freedom and equal rights. Now the simple people of remote villages knew words like democracy and human rights; expressions like freedom and equality. They were not some abstract concepts for somebody somewhere far away in America or Western Europe. They had been awakened to rights they had been denied, and they were ready to pursue them.

It was a clear September night, like the summer nights I remembered from my childhood when I reached out and connected to the universe. Old enemies Kanlı and Hasan were sitting next to each other. Once bitter rivals over a piece of land, now the old animosity was forgotten. There was a larger and meaner enemy they needed to fight together. There were young men and old toothless men who all laughed and smiled at the fact that one of them made it to the other side of the Iron Curtain and returned. In their eyes, I was a great success because I not only managed to escape, but I had made it to America, a country for which all of them had great respect because it stood up for their rights in a moment of need.

I was saddened that I could not see Mustafa's parents in the crowd. I wanted to meet them, but at the same time I was overwrought with anxiety because I didn't know how to approach them to tell them how sorry I was about Mustafa's demise.

That night I was ecstatic to see Hasan, even though he had aged a lot. But something in his eyes was the same; he was a man with inner strength. He had decided to do something to stop and reverse the name change campaign. A group of more educated Turks, Hasan and Rafet mualim included, decided to organize a peaceful demonstration in Krumovgrad for the reversal of the name change campaign. Unfortunately, the secret police had managed to plant an informant in the group, and they were all arrested, taken into police custody and severely beaten by half a dozen masked police officers. The next day they were loaded onto a narrow, dark police truck and driven to a faraway island on the Danube River, to the notorious Belene concentration camp. Many Turks who resisted the name change campaign spent time there from 1985 until 1989, under most inhumane conditions. Hasan told me what he had endured, from standing barefoot on ice in the winter to the random beatings from the guards.

During the conversation with the villagers, I still detected worry among these Turks who were trapped behind the Iron Curtain. What would happen to them? Would they be successful in their efforts to regain their rights in Bulgaria without bloodshed? These simple people were no longer sheep the Communists could manipulate any way they wanted. There was a determination inside them. These people were knowledgeable about human rights and democracy. There was real growth in their thinking, largely because of the Western radio broadcasts.

That night I told my father I would like to visit my grandparents. He looked at me somberly and said that they both had passed away shortly after the name change campaign, one after the other. I was greatly saddened that I would not be able to see my beloved grandparents again. I still was going to visit their graves and the old house, where I had spent my childhood summers, and say goodbye.

Chapter 25

The next day I decided to face my biggest fear, which had been a part of me for the last five years. Would I be blamed by Mustafa's parents for his demise? I told my parents that I was going to see Mustafa's parents and they said it was the right thing to do. I hoped that they could wash away the guilt which had been eating at me for so long. I had been carrying the guilt like a heavy burden around my neck for too long. It slowed me down and hindered my advance in life. I knew that facing Mustafa's parents would be the toughest thing I have ever done. I dreaded the moment, but I could not move ahead without their blessing or forgiveness. I could not imagine the devastating pain Mustafa's parents had gone through, losing their beloved son. I remembered the love and care with which his mother spoke to Mustafa when he was leaving for school.

I walked slowly along the cobblestone narrow road, small stone houses to my left and right. My feet took me slowly to Mustafa's parents' house. By the time I reached it, all the energy in my body had drained away and I felt weak, my head swimming in a fog. I reached their outside yard door and I could see that there was no one in the yard. The place had not changed at all during my time away. I went inside the courtyard to the door and knocked. Mustafa's sister appeared. She was about 11 years old now and I didn't know whether she remembered me.

"Could I speak to your parents?" I asked her.

"Yes," she said shyly, turning to alert her parents to a visitor.

I waited for a minute, then the door slowly opened and Mustafa's father came out and, after him, Mustafa's mother.

"Selamun aleykum," I said, my throat dry from anxiety and unease.

"Aleykum selam," they said, one after another. They looked aged beyond their fifties.

Mustafa's father approached me and extended his hand and put his other hand on my shoulder and looked me in the eyes. He could not talk because he was gripped by an immense emotional pain. He barely could say "Welcome, son." Then Mustafa's mother hugged me and started crying. Slowly the hope and realization that I was not blamed for the death of their only son emerged like the light through a curtain slowly pulled open during a sunny day.

It was still difficult to master words because of the anxiety gripping my throat.

"Do you blame me for Mustafa's death?" I asked.

"No," they quickly said in unison.

Inside I was like a coiled spring suddenly released. My tears came swiftly and the only thing I was able to say again and again was, "I am sorry for Mustafa's death. Please forgive me. Mustafa saved my life; if not for him I would be dead."

"There is nothing to forgive," Mustafa's father said. "Hasan told us that it was Mustafa's decision to follow you. He told us that you didn't want Mustafa to go with you because it was dangerous." He wiped tears from his face with his hand. "My son, we never blamed you. We were sad that fate decided Mustafa had to die, but we never blamed you. We blamed the Communists who forced you to escape to save your life."

I knew they were sincere. They were simple people; I knew them well enough to know they were free of pretense. Generous and pure souls — fate was so cruel to these kind people. I lifted my head and looked at the whitewashed wall and I saw one single, black-and-white picture of Mustafa smiling, expecting only goodness in life.

The knowledge that I was not blamed helped me gather myself together. I started feeling better, and a weight lifted from my chest. I had been suffering for so long because I believed that I should suffer, that I deserved it. The tears of remorse had cleansed me, and I understood that there was no reason to feel guilty, although it didn't stop me from feeling emotional pain for these two pure souls in front of me. My mind started to see the world differently, less threatening. My appreciation toward these simple people, Mustafa's parents, my own parents, and all the villagers in Çaliköy, grew.

Chapter 26

On the third day I decided to go to Krumovgrad. I traveled by bus, leaving from the same bus stop on the road where I had arrived two days prior. The slow bus took me through winding roads toward the town. When we approached, I saw the red roofs of the houses. My first thought was it had not changed at all during the last five years, except it looked more neglected. Weeds grew everywhere; stray dogs and farm animals roamed freely on the streets, abandoned when their owners fled for Turkey. Most of the buildings needed a fresh coat of paint and sidewalks needed repair.

I also felt a certain uneasiness among the Bulgarian population. They had information from their relatives who were party functionaries that the name change would be reversed and they would be the minority in an area mostly populated by Turks. There was no reason to be anxious—the name change campaign had been initiated by the ruling Communist regime, not by the Bulgarian population. There was no reason for any tension between the two communities. There was growing belief among the local population that the restitution of the Turkish names was a question of time.

The town was mostly the same as I remembered it. There was a warm and pleasant fall breeze and the yellow and orange colored poplar leaves greeted me with "Welcome back, Osman." It felt good to be back, even though many people were gone. There were people around, but I didn't recognize most of them. They must be the people who moved from the villages to the town after the exodus that summer.

I was walking around the sales stalls when I glimpsed somebody I knew from before, although he had aged way too much for just five years.

"Merhaba Rafet mualim," I said, approaching him. My teacher who had been in his middle thirties was now in his forties. He looked bewildered, studied me a long time, and then his face slowly brightened. I could see that he was shocked and emotionally affected by our meeting.

"How are you Rafet mualim?" I asked before he had chance to respond and grabbed his hand and shook it hard.

"I am well, but, Osman is that really you?" he said, unable to shake the expression of surprise from his face.

"Yes, Rafet mualim. I am Osman, your former student."

"It is great to see you. I heard that you and Mustafa had been shot on the Bulgarian-Greek border," he said, still puzzled.

"That's what the Communists told you and if you believed them, they told you half of the truth. Unfortunately, they managed to kill Mustafa." My gaze shifted from Rafet's face to the ground. I felt pangs of sadness and guilt gripping me inside. The black monster was threatening to throw the blanket of darkness over me again, wiping the smile from my face.

"That's what everyone was saying," Rafet said.

"I guess everybody was wrong. I guess without me there to prove that I was alive it was easy to deceive everybody," I replied. "Are you still a teacher in the local high school?" I wanted to change the attention from me to Rafet and stop the feeling of sadness that was threatening to engulf me.

"No, I have not been a teacher for long time," he said, his face turning serious, almost stern. "I and a few other intellectuals from the town organized a small resistance group immediately after the name change campaign ended in 1985. We wanted to organize the local Turkish population to peacefully resist the forceful assimilation policies of the Bulgarian Communist Party. Unfortunately we didn't know that there was a spy among us, and one morning I was awakened by a bunch of police officers. They put a hood over my head and I ended up in cell in the police station where I was beaten by group of police officers who all wore face masks. From there I was transported to Belene concentration camp where I spend the last five years, until the regime decided to open the border with Turkey."

Rafet paused, deep in thought, and I remembered Hasan being in this group of prisoners beaten and sent to Belene.

"I was forced to leave the country in May," Rafet continued, "and I was taken to the Svilengrad border gate. I spent all summer in a refugee camp in Turkey, but toward the end of the summer I realized that Turkey would not be able to take all the Turks of Bulgaria. I thought hard and long about the plight of our minority and realized that we should be able to live in our place of birth. We have been living in these lands for many generations, half a millennium, and we have the right to live in peaceful coexistence with the Bulgarian majority. So at the end of summer, when there were rumors circulating in the refugee camps that the Turks were going to close the border because they were unable to cope with the inflow of refugees, I decided to return to Bulgaria and work for the rights of the local Turks. Now we are in the process of establishing a political party which will defend the interests of the Turkish and Muslim minorities in Bulgaria. We believe that soon there will be many political parties in Bulgaria. Now there is no power tha can stop the advance of democracy and freedom, the path leads only one way — for greater democracy. We believe that this trend is irreversible."

"The change in the thinking of the people is amazing," I said. "The people of Bulgaria were treated like cattle; they were not allowed to think with their own heads, and now everybody talks about freedom and democracy. Now is the right time for change here. I realize it took a long time for people to adopt these ideas, but they have been brutally oppressed by the regime for too long. They have been contained within the boundaries of Bulgaria and no effort has been spared by the rulers to cut people's connection with the outside world, to keep them uninformed so they could manipulate them any way they want."

I was happy to meet and talk with Rafet. He was one of the true harbingers of change and democracy this country needed. And I was very happy to be able to come back and see my place of birth. Above all, I was impressed with the people's desire for change. But I was also happy and ready to go back to Turkey, so I could travel back to the USA with my fiancée.

Chapter 27

After paying a hefty fine on the Bulgarian border for not getting the required stamps and hotel receipts, I made it back to Turkey in one piece. I went straight to my aunt's house in Istanbul. I could not wait to see Leyla and head for America with my fiancée. My aunt was happy to see me, and she asked about my parents, how they were. I told her that they were fine and I brought her some of the plums from my grandparents' orchard that she would often repeat she loved and missed. She was happy to get the plums. Then she looked at me seriously, almost grim, and said, "Sit down. I have news to tell you about Leyla." I was puzzled, not sure what to think.

"What?" I managed to say, a sinking feeling spreading to my gut.

"One day when you were away in Bulgaria, a young lady stopped at our house. She rang the doorbell, and I went to see who was there. I saw a young lady I had not seen before, and she said, 'I have news from Leyla for Osman. Are you his aunt?'" And I said, "Yes, I am Osman's aunt, what is the matter?"

She said she was a friend of Leyla, who sent her here to tell you that her parents found the immigration papers and took them from her. They are upset with her and they have prohibited her from leaving the house. The friend said Leyla still loves Osman, but she doesn't know what to do, she is trapped at their house. Her parents took her passport and papers; even if she escapes, she cannot leave with Osman without them.

Then my aunt said, "I am sorry that this is happening, but maybe we did something wrong. We should not try to be sneaky about your connection with Leyla. We needed to let Leyla's parents know about Leyla's and your love. Now we have to do it the hard way, but the right way. I will go with my husband and visit Leyla's parents and try to persuade them to allow the two of you to get married. I know it i as long shot, but maybe we will be able to change their minds."

I was stunned to hear all this about Leyla. I could not believe it, my world was falling apart. Just when I thought that I was all set to leave, this had to happen. I was bewildered — now there was that uncertainty again. I didn't know what to think, but I was grateful to my aunt for her willingness to help. She was a shrewd and smart lady. If anyone could fix this, she could.

My aunt went to see Leyla at her parents' home. She came back grim-faced and I was instantly gripped with fear and anxiety. I knew that something bad had happened. My aunt sighed and looked at me and said, "I am sorry to tell you this but Leyla is very sick. She has a fever and she cannot eat. Her parents told me she tries to eat, but she cannot hold food down, she throws up. This is not good. Leyla's parents had the doctor come to see her. He said that she suffers from fatigue and exhaustion."

"What do you think Leyla is suffering from, aunt?" I asked anxiously.

"I know exactly what it is and what the cure is," she said and looked straight at me. "You are the cure."

"What do you mean, I am the cure?"

"I know exactly what Leyla is suffering from."

"What is it?" I asked impatiently

"Osman, she is lovesick. I have no doubt in my mind that she is suffering a bad case of lovesickness."

"How do you know that?"

"Because she was fine when you left for Bulgaria," said my aunt with a serious expression on her face. "She had the passport and fiancée visa ready to go. She was waiting for you to come back from Bulgaria so she could go with you to the U.S. She was seeing the other man to please her parents, but she didn't love him, she always loved you. Now when suddenly her hopes are dashed, she has become ill."

"I think I need to go and see Leyla," I said, feeling sick myself.

"I think you should wait for an invitation," my aunt replied in a stern voice. "Don't push your luck."

"What if the invitation is not forthcoming?" I asked, anxiety eating at me inside.

"That will be bad, but I don't think you should lose all hope," she said with certainty.

"Why are you saying that I shouldn't lose hope?" I said with despair. She sighed.

"When I visited Leyla's family, Leyla's mother told me that when Leyla was delirious she repeated your name. If Leyla's parents decide that a visit from you could help Leyla to recover, I would think that invitation could be soon on its way." There was certainty in her voice.

"Do you really believe that they would invite me to their home to see

Leyla, or are you just trying to soothe me?" I asked, seeing a little ray of hope in the darkness.

"Osman, if I had a daughter lovesick like Leyla I would not hesitate even for one minute. I would let the man whom my daughter loves into my house immediately. But that's me. I cannot predict how Leyla's parents will react. Now, I have a plan. I don't know whether it will work, but we have to try. I will go and talk to Leyla's parents. I will tell them about your relationship. I will suggest to them that maybe you going and seeing Leyla could be good for her. I hope I can persuade them to see things our way."

*   *   *

The next day my aunt went to meet with Leyla's parents again. I waited with hope and desperation, fighting a war inside me. I didn't know what to do or think. One minute I had hope, the next I was plunged into desperation. I could not understand why this was happening and I waited in uncertainty. My aunt came back from her visit and sought me out in the living room where I was watching television.

"Osman!" she announced triumphantly. "Tomorrow we are going to see Leyla!"

I could not believe what I was hearing. I jumped up and enveloped my aunt in a hug, so happy was I to hear the news.

Once I let her go, my aunt continued her news. "We have been invited to visit Leyla and her family, but be careful not to talk too much. I apologized to Leyla's parents for keeping them in the dark about your connection with her, and it would be a good idea if you apologized, too. It seems that they are worried about their daughter, they are desperate, and they are willing to try anything so Leyla gets better."

The next day we took a cab to Leyla's house. My aunt knew where Leyla's house was situated and gave instructions to the cab driver. We stopped in the front of the house and pushed the doorbell. A grim-faced woman in her sixties, Leyla's mother, opened the door. We exchanged greetings and were invited into their living room, which didn't look bad for people who had just moved to Turkey this summer. I met with Leyla's father, who was soft-spoken. Then we were invited into Leyla's room.

There, lying in the bed, was my love. She was so pale, I was afraid that she was terminally ill and was never going to recover. She was my wilting rose. We sat on chairs opposite Leyla's bed. Leyla's mother went to her and gently touched her face and forehead and said, "My child, you have guests. You need to wake up and see them."

For a moment, I thought Leyla would not open her eyes, but slowly she did. She turned her gaze toward me and she just looked at me for a moment. Then a faint smile spread across her face.

"Osman," she said quietly and slowly, and I think she tried to extend her hand.

"Leyla," I responded, and got up from the chair and approached her and took her soft hand in my own. "How are you, Leyla?"

"I am better now that I see you," she replied softly.

"Please get better," I pleaded with her.

"I will if you promise to come and see me," she said.

"I will do whatever you ask me to," I said, choking back tears.

Then Leyla lay back. I think she was too tired to talk. We all sat in that room in silence for a while. Too soon, my aunt thought we should leave. My tireless aunt kept in touch with Leyla's family, and we went the next day to see Leyla. She looked better, and she was able to eat and she expressed a desire to see me again. I was happy to see her as she made slow but steady progress toward health. My aunt was able to convince Leyla's mother that my presence nurtured Leyla to health, and she also hinted that we should be united in marriage since we loved each other so much. Leyla's mother responded positively, and she was able to convince her husband to agree to our marriage. My aunt and Leyla's mother agreed on a date for when my aunt would officially request Leyla's hand for me, and that day would be our modest engagement party. I bought two lovely gold rings. We had the engagement party with a few neighbors invited, and a nice meal in Leyla's house. With Leyla's health markedly improved, she was almost like her previous self.

Our wedding was modest, with my aunt Zeynep and her husband Jafer present, Leyla's parents, and a few neighbors. Now there was nothing to stop us. I announced to Leyla's parents that we would be leaving soon for America. They were sad that they would be separated from their daughter, but they were glad she was healthy and in good spirits. Finally, I bought two one-way tickets from Istanbul to Chicago.

My new bride and I left to begin our lives together in the new world.

Epilogue

I thought long and hard about my experiences when I came back to America with my new wife, my beloved Leyla. No matter what life throws our way we have the capacity, or we can develop the capacity, to overcome anything. We have the ability to shape our lives the way we want. This is not something I came up with, this is how our universe functions.

Nowadays, I don't worry very much about the past. I live in the present, since my present is the past of my future. I work hard in the present to build a successful future in my new adopted country. Every slice of present time is a slice of eternity. That's how we taste eternity.

Gradually, I started viewing myself as more than just a Turk from Bulgaria. I adopted the view that I am a citizen of the world, a global soul.

Author's Notes

I was born in Krumovgrad, a small town in southern Bulgaria near Greece. I am a member of the Turkish minority of Bulgaria, who are descendants of the Ottoman Turks who ruled Bulgaria for half a millennium. I graduated from Vasil Levski High School in Krumovgrad. After high school I served my compulsory two-year military service in Bulgaria, where members of all minorities were utilized as free slave labor. There were Gypsies, Pomaks, Turks of course, and many Bulgarians who had criminal backgrounds or had relatives in the West, which was frowned upon. We weren't trusted with the supposed sophisticated weaponry of the military of the advanced socialism, as the rulers called their form of government. We were assigned Mannliher rifles from the time of World War I. Since we were working all the time, 10-12 hour days, 6 sometimes 7 days a week without being paid, our rifles were kept in storage. We were told that we would have to defend the open coal mines, where we were building railroads for the trains moving the coal and earth. We were going to defend the coal mines with the Mannlihers against invading Americans and the rest of NATO, who would came after us with F-16s and Abraham Tanks. Good luck to us.

Not long after I was discharged from the military, the notorious name change campaign was initiated by the leadership of the Bulgarian Communist Party. The campaign started slowly in 1983, but really accelerated in the fall of 1984. It moved like a slow-burning fire from the most southeastern part of the country in the fall and winter of 1984, to the north and west in the winter of 1985. The Turks living east and south of Krumovgrad were forced to change their names in an attempt on the part of authorities to eradicate Turkish culture in their country. For resisting the name change campaign, some Turks were viciously attacked and beaten and their valuables were taken from them. Some were sent to prisons and others to the notorious concentration camp in the island of Belene. In the middle of the night, villages would be surrounded by military police and paramilitary, and Turks were forced at gunpoint to have their names changed from Turkish to Bulgarian.

When my father saw what happened to the Turks living south and east of Krumovgrad, he decided not to resist. He was warned privately by his friend, the chief of police in town, and also by an official in the Communist Party of our province, that resistance was futile. He could not escape from the inevitable, they told him. The names of all Turks in Bulgaria would be changed and he should not resist, for his own good. Before

214

the name change he had been friends with these men, despite their cultural differences. The actions of the ruling government, meant to unite the country under one ethnicity, only managed to drive a wedge between men like my father and his former friends. When my father was told that it was our turn to go through the name change, he took the passports of all in our household and gave them to the clerks working in the savet, the equivalent of the town hall in the States. That is how our names were changed from Turkish to Bulgarian in the fall of 1984. I could not forget all these events of the name change campaign and I was compelled to write the book *Crack in the Curtain*.

This book is a judgment against a Communist political regime and its dictator, Todor Zhivkov, whose name change campaign against ethnic Turks initiated and facilitated crimes against humanity.

It is this author's privilege to have known many good Bulgarians and to have mostly great memories from the country where he was born and raised. This book is by no means a judgment or criticism of the Bulgarian people, who themselves were oppressed by the Communist regime. The majority of Eastern European people were robbed not only of acquiring material wealth, but also of their right to spiritual faith — faith in God — which is such a substantial part of the lives of the people living in free societies.

All the violence perpetrated against the Turks living in Bulgaria had the opposite effect sought by the BCP. Communist rulers had wanted to eradicate Islam, since the basic canon of the Communist party is atheism. After the names of Turks were reconstituted by the new Bulgarian government in 1990, however, Islam was strengthened in Bulgaria. More fascinating information is available on my blog: www.selatinsofta.com.

Historical Comments

The systematic, forceful campaign of assimilating ethnic and religious minorities in Bulgaria was begun by the Communist party after they came to power in 1944. Until the Bulgarian Communist name change campaign in 1984-1985, ethnic Turks remaining within the boundaries of Bulgaria had been able to keep their language, religion, and customs mostly intact. Rapid growth of the Turkish population in the early 1980s, however, compared with stagnant numbers of the Bulgarian majority, worried the leaders of the Bulgarian Communist Party. The rapid solution for this "problem" was to assimilate the ethnic Turkish minority into the Bulgarian nation by any means necessary, including the use of force against the Turks and the conversion of their

Turkish names to Bulgarian. The name change campaign , however, failed to eradicate Turkish identity.

A great number of Turks remained in the northeastern part of Bulgaria after the Russian-Ottoman War of 1878. The south central part of Bulgaria was added to the country from the Ottoman Empire in 1912-1913 after the Balkan wars. This is where the ancestors of the author of this book have lived for many generations. In October 1912, war was declared against the Ottoman Empire by Bulgaria, Serbia, Greece, and Montenegro. These allied armies easily conquered almost all the European part of the Ottoman Empire. Bulgaria did not agree to divide Macedonia among Greece, Serbia, and Bulgaria, and instead claimed all Macedonia as Bulgarian territory.

On June 16, 1913, Bulgaria attacked Greece, Serbia, and Montenegro, and the second Balkan War started. Because of the greed, uncompromising stance, and lack of foresight of the Bulgarian rulers, Bulgaria lost the war. Then the Ottoman Empire attacked Bulgaria from the south, and Romania attacked Bulgaria from the north. The Ottoman Empire was able to take back Edirne and eastern Thrace, which are situated in the European part of modern Turkey. Shortly after the second Balkan War, World War I broke out and Bulgaria was one of the nations defeated. Bulgaria was punished by losing access to the Aegean Sea and ceding the southern Rhodope Mountains to Greece.